CURSED & CREEPY

CURSED & CREEPY

TRAILERS, TATTOOS, & FERRIS WHEELS+++

THE HORROR LITE SERIES
BOOK 1

ANGELIQUE FAWNS   AKIS LINARDOS

SHANNON FOX   ROBERT STAHL   R.J.K. LEE

CHRISTOPHER HENCKEL

CONTENTS

FOREWORD

DON'T LET HER CHARMS FOOL YOU

BY MARK LESLIE

Don't let the brilliant sparkle in her eye, nor the radiant and beautiful smile Angelique Fawns greets you with fool you. Don't let the woman's open, personable, and welcoming persona, nor the pleasant tone of her upbeat voice deceive you the way I was so masterfully misled.

Her imagination and her stories are creepy as hell.

It's hidden brilliantly beneath the surface—below that delightfully warm and positive demeanor. Hidden so subtly within the notes of her contagious melodic laugh.

Let this be your warning now, dear reader.

This woman will curse you something fierce.

She will leave you haunted with images, characters, settings, and situations that will return to you in the dead of night. And, as you cower beneath the covers, panicking at every little sound that echoes through the thick dark night, your mind returning to . . .

. . . the haunting eerie artwork discovered in a bitter dry desert . . .

BY MARK LESLIE

. . . the disturbing chills that echo through the blades of a bedroom fan on an unbearably humid, hot, and sticky summer night . . .

. . . a cursed trailer that twists and flips a stereotype into something darkly humorous . . .

. . . of a haunted Ferris Wheel that beckons with exciting promises of thrills from better times . . .

. . . a mysterious hidden tattoo shop where the ink is laced with more than a unique and bold hue . . .

. . . serpentine revenge served like the refrain from a shock rock song . . .

. . . the power of harmonic notes that mask an unspeakable mayhem . . .

. . . you will rue the day that you fell prey to her irresistible charms.

But don't just take my word for it. Within the pages of this book, you'll see how Akis Linardos, Shannon Fox, R.J.K. Lee, Robert Stahl, and Christopher Henckel all fell victim in similar ways to me. Angelique roped them in to share their own horrors. Their curses are evident in the tales they were compelled to share here:

Of an evil cursed ink with a motive darker than its pitch black hue; of a collectibles shop where the sale offered up is a price you can't refuse; a vengeful pumpkin with a sinister glare and something dangerous lurking behind its jagged, crescent-moon grin; of the disturbing terror beneath what is to so many others a beloved and magical night; and of an eerie carnival that offers up more chills than thrills.

For the love of all things holy, I implore you to stop reading now; for something wicked lingers in the pages you are about to traverse.

Do not let Angelique's compelling offer to bend your ear with her deviously dark tales tempt you.

Or, if like me, and like the other authors you'll find among these cursed pages, you pay no heed to my warnings, and venture forth, know this one thing: you will be forever changed, and these stories will haunt you, will linger on the edges of your imagination, and will return to you in those dark and quiet moments when you think you're all alone in the thick black of night.

But know this: you won't be.

Angelique Fawns will be there with you, grinning at you in that delightful and welcoming way that drew you in the first place.

Welcoming you back to the creepy cursed worlds of hers that will ever linger in your mind, your heart, your very soul.

Mark Leslie

October 2023

1

ABOUT "KUTULU IN THE DESERT"

∽

First published: October 2022
DreamForge Magazine

THIS STORY WAS INSPIRED by the art of Dale Chihuly, a glass artist whose work is eerie and exceptional. Almost alien...

2

KUTULU IN THE DESERT

BY ANGELIQUE FAWNS

The Humvee shudders as it drives over the Sonoran Desert. What used to be a stretch of soaring cacti is now desolate and charred. An eagle flying overhead attempts to gain altitude, its talons glowing purple. Penny pulls over and climbs onto the hood, reloading her weapon. She aims at the struggling bird of prey. Summoning a sense of calm and purpose, she pulls the trigger.

~

Two Days Earlier:

The Arizona sun beats down on Penny as she uses tongs to hold the pad of the Prickly Pear plant and snips at the joint. The cactus is wilting and dropping spines onto the Cave Creek Botanical Garden walkway. Her uniform is so sweaty it sticks to her back and her skin itches. This job is the first time she's worn something other than pajamas or sweatpants in almost two years.

Fastidiously, she sweeps up every last needle. It wouldn't do to

3

have a tourist's foot pierced when the garden opens in two days for the big art show. She pauses to tuck an errant curl back under her green ball cap that says "US Army Tank Corp" and enjoy the silence. No people. No noise. No traffic. The tight lines around her eyes relax and a smile tickles her lips.

"*Kutulu in the Desert: Art Meets Nature*" banners decorate the park. She watches a hummingbird buzz between the colorful sculptures that twist toward the sky. There are six structures in all, glittering among the native Sonoran Desert plants. A cloud passes over the sun. The tiny bird is cast in shadow several feet under a Kutulu tube. Penny's breath catches. She wants to pluck the creature out of the air and keep it safe in her pocket. Shaking the moment off, she takes a deep breath of a flowering Creosote Bush, enjoying the earthy smell.

"This sure beats the odour of stale wine," Penny says to the hummingbird.

The iridescent green blur doesn't stick around; fluttering up into the pasta-like yellow Kutulu. A bang makes Penny jump and drop the broom.

Her supervisor Oliver slams his coffee cup down again on the table in his administrative tent. "Penny, hurry it up! Your shift ended five minutes ago."

He'd been loading firecrackers onto a trolley for the party planned for opening night. Oliver is built like a barrel cactus, everything about him short and squat. His coke bottle glasses make his eyes appear comically large.

"Don't rush the process Oliver, good things take time." Penny's cheeks flush.

Oliver leaves his tent and trundles over to Penny. "I'm trying to be patient."

"I've learned the hard way to double-check." She picks up a water bottle to squirt a Desert Honeysuckle, trying to control the tremble in her hand.

Oliver's face contorts in rage. "You know what I'm learning about the hard way? These dang veteran employment programs."

"You'd prefer a pimply teenager that does a half-ass job?"

Oliver speaks like he's talking to an infant. "If you stay late, I can't do what I need to do. Finish up!"

Pulling her ball cap low to hide tears, she concentrates on the hummingbird. It's flitting around the orange Kutulu. She listens to the buzz of the impossibly fast wings. Penny takes a deep breath and goes back to her trimming when a curly piece of Kutulu moves.

She blinks.

The tube shifts, quivering. It moves closer to the hummingbird. With a lightening quick strike, it sucks the bird in. A thrashing lump travels through the length of the glistening arm and disappears into the trunk.

Penny rubs her eyes. *What did she just see? The Kutulu just ate the hummingbird?*

"I said, finish up!" Oliver grabs her elbow.

"Don't touch me, you crap hat!" Penny jerks away from him, balling up her fists.

"What did you call me?"

"I didn't mean to name call. But that thing-" She points a tremulous hand at the Kutulu. "-just ate the hummingbird."

Oliver wrinkles his nose. "You must have sunstroke. Time to go home."

Penny shuts her eyes and counts to ten. A technique her therapist taught her.

Oliver is so close she can smell his coffee breath. "Ignore me, will you? Are you looking to get fired?"

She tries not to let her revulsion show.

"I'm sorry. I am so, so sorry. I will do anything. Please, I need this job. I'll work faster. I really, really need this job." She claws at him.

Oliver backs away. "Calm down. Consider this a warning. It takes a special sort of person to work here, not everyone assimilates. Go home and get a good night's sleep."

Penny nods and gathers up her tools. A headache blooms behind her eyebrows.

Could the vanishing hummingbird simply be explained by an oncoming migraine? She's trying to fit in so badly, she might be stress hallucinating.

She hurries past the award-winning visitor's center with its bright Aztec tiles and stained-glass windows. A pond full of Koi fish sparkles in the courtyard. Guests never see the tired gardening shed hidden near the garbage dumpsters.

Cracking open the door, the smell of old diesel, manure, and dust tickles her nostrils. Penny flicks the switch, but the room stays dark. Using the bit of light from a big dusty window, she places her toolbelt on a shelf. A beam of mote-filled sun illuminates a bag of fertilizer and several jerry cans of fuel in the corner. She sucks in her breath. The bag is chock full of ammonium nitrogen. Combine that chemical with gas and you have one dandy of a bomb.

She doesn't dare go back and talk to Oliver about it today.

On the short drive home, she smokes the one cigarette she allows herself. The box of matches and menthol cancer stick sit in her pocket all day waiting for this one moment. Inhaling deeply, she lets the nicotine relax her nerves.

***

Penny draws the curtains on her apartment window to block out the early morning sun. Sipping coffee slowly, she types with one hand on her laptop. The Cave Creek Botanical Garden website is full of hype about the upcoming exhibition, but low on facts.

"Kutulu in the Desert is a new exhibition set against majestic cacti and the Sonoran Desert.

Come see the work of O. Kutulu and his groundbreaking pieces that combine art and

architecture."

That's it. No more info on the artist. Not even a picture.

A Google search brings up a blurb about an art show in New York. It's from five years ago and featured an O. Kutulu and his remarkable blown glass creations. Next item is an abstract from the University of Miami about a "Kutulu" involved in a failed nano-technology experiment.

An alarm reminds her it's time to go to work. Her car keys sit beside a photo of seven soldiers posing with a UH-60 Blackhawk Helicopter. She's in the center while the rest of her crew are grinning and flashing peace signs. Her coffee turns acidic in her stomach but Penny still packs her cigarette and climbs into her surplus military vehicle.

At work she tries to tell Oliver about the improperly stored fertilizer in the gardening shed.

He interrupts her. "Look at those plants crowding the art installations! Get your trimmers and cut back the cacti. It looks sloppy."

Penny's jaw drops. The orange Kutulu is bloated and each twisty arm is thicker. A nearby Agave plant is dehydrated.

"The plants aren't doing the crowding." She points to an organ pipe cactus, half the arms severed by a blue Kutulu. "The art pieces are larger."

"Aren't they beautiful? Don't they call to you?" Oliver shocks her by smiling.

"They're... interesting," Penny stutters.

"That's all you have to say? Interesting? Listen to them." He looks at her expectantly.

"I hear nothing. And they grew."

"Are we going to have more problems today?" Oliver doesn't wait for an answer, heading for his tent.

Penny grabs some equipment from the storage shed, but first takes a moment to move the gas cans as far from the fertilizer bags as the small room allows. Outside, the sun warms her cheeks and a cool breeze almost whips off her ball cap. After tightening the back of it, she looks at the dying plants.

"Penny.... work!" Oliver watches her from the tent.

She wades in with a shovel and digs out an Agave.

"Terrible waste of Tequila." She tosses the mutilated plant.

"What did you say?"

"Nothing."

Penny grabs a saw and carefully cuts off Saguaro limbs. Wiping sweat from her brow, she considers the last Kutulu installation to clean up. This one is a formation of ebony spikes sprouting from a flat round ball. Frowning, she notices some of the tubes are arching over the walkway. The ends look dangerous. Using the saw, she knocks the protruding pieces off.

An enraged shriek comes from the tent and Oliver bursts out. "What did you do? Are you crazy?"

"We have to keep this place safe for the public. Think of the lawsuit if someone gets impaled by a tube."

He waves a stubby fist. "Look I don't know what kind of PTSD is making you a lunatic, but that was a priceless piece of art."

"What do you know about PTSD? Maybe the only reason you have your cushy supervisor job is because I defended our country."

"What makes you think I'm a supervisor?" Oliver's spit speckles her face.

Penny wipes her cheek. "Sorry, should I call you Overlord of the Garden?"

Oliver stomps. "You have no respect for the Kutulu. You're fired!"

"Are you sure you can fire me? Isn't there a board of directors or--?"

Her words trail off when she sees the decapitated Kutulu tube curl up with a hiss. Red smoke wafts from the black damaged end.

"Get out! Leave now. Before I charge you with vandalism." Oliver waves a fist.

"Did you not see that?"

"Get out!"

Saw still dangling from her hand, Penny walks back to her Humvee. And drives. Her hands are shaking so much she can't even light her one cigarette. Her ears buzz. Like when her squadron got blown up. The same buzz. The same feeling of dissociation. If she'd only seen the landmine earlier...

She pulls over to the side of the road and concentrates on her breathing. Every time she tries to belong somewhere she blows it up. Oxygen in. Carbon Dioxide out. Her eye catches the sticker on her sunshade.

Duty before Death.

She reaches into the center console, originally used for ammunition, but now repurposed as her travelling apothecary. The bottle of

Diazepam is stained and well-handled. She dry swallows a pill and clenches her steering wheel. It takes a few moments, but her panic subsides.

Duty before Death, she reads the slogan she slapped on the truck when she was still serving.

There's a cold bottle of Pinot Grigio, her sweat pants, and Netflix waiting for her at home.

Penny rests her head on her white-knuckled hands.

She didn't imagine that hummingbird being sucked into the Kutulu tube yesterday. The fact they're growing... no art she knows of does that. And what kind of monstrous creation hisses and curls up when trimmed?

Flipping down the visor and opening the mirror, Penny talks to her reflection. "You may be a discharged American soldier, but you are still a soldier. I don't know what's going on at that garden, but it could be a threat to the citizens of the United States. The country you swore to protect. Put on your big girl panties!"

Penny turns the car around and drives back to the Botanical Garden. This time she doesn't park in the lot. Let's see Oliver intimidate her when she roars up in a Humvee. She learned a few things in the army. Like you need the element of surprise if you want the upper hand on your enemy. She gains confidence from the power of the massive military vehicle, some of the old "Hooah!" in her veins. She drives into the main court yard -- and has to rub her eyes.

There is a new Kutulu sprouting out of the pond. Purple, red and blue twists reach for the cloudless sky. They're growing out of a huge trunk, as wide as a California Redwood. Standing on the rock border rock, Oliver gestures like a conductor. A stream of purple shoots from his fingertips.

Penny figures it out. *O. Kutulu. Oliver Kutulu. The artist AND the scientist.*

His chubby body jitters as he creates. A slurping sound accompanies the formation of the new Kutulu. This is the most massive, colorful one yet. The other Kutulu hum and sway in the cool breeze coming down from the nearby mountains. Sweat streams from Oliver's forehead and the liquid material continues to flow from his hands. Purple changes to orange.

She hops out of her Humvee, saw in one hand, and strides to the edge of the pond. "Oliver."

He changes the stream of orange to red, his eyes never leaving the Kutulu.

"Oliver!" Penny pokes him in the butt cheek with the tip of the saw.

He falls off the rock border with a startled bray and the stream from his fingertips abruptly ceases. The last bits of red fluid harden to globs and bounce on the crushed stone path. Pebble-sized bits smack Penny in the face and arms. They sizzle on her skin, leaving something akin to a bug bite.

She holds her breath, looking at the spot on her arm where the largest one hit. Her skin is red and tingles. Her brain gives a sudden jolt, like the one time she sniffed a line of coke during her tour of duty.

Oliver pulls himself up, brushing off his khaki pants. "You're like a bad rash."

Penny points her saw at his head. "What the actual eff?"

"Go home. Forget you saw anything here. You're hallucinating." Oliver's lips don't move.

Penny blinks rapidly. "Something is happening, but I don't think I'm hallucinating."

"Go home, Penny. Come back for the opening tomorrow. Everything is okay." Oliver's voice massages her cerebral cortex.

Penny can feel herself nodding, she loosens her fingers on her saw. "Why can I hear you in my brain?"

Oliver raises his eyebrow, lips still pressed together. "Because I'm trying to communicate with you telepathically. This is how I talk with the Kutulu. I had no idea someone like you had the talent. I can teach you. We don't have to be enemies."

"It's like a mind tickle."

A wide grin transforms Oliver's face into something almost pleasant. "Stay and help me get the garden ready." He gestures at the new Kutulu.

It rustles, almost as if in greeting, then dips one purple tendril into the pond and sucks up a shimmering Koi. Penny can see the wiggling fish travelling down the opaque tube. She feels a brief rush of pleasure, as if she just ate a particularly tasty candy. She gives her head a violent shake and severs whatever connection she had to Oliver and his carnivorous art.

"What's really going on here Oliver?" She jabs the saw at his soft belly.

Oliver sucks in his gut, but doesn't retreat. "Haven't you always wanted to belong, Penny? Isn't that why you joined the army? You need purpose. A family. If you won't leave, you might as well join us."

His voice and eyes are like a promised vacation. The magnified pupils deep and warm.

"Belong to what?" She lets the saw fall to the ground and steps closer to her boss.

"This." Oliver gestures at the Kutulu gleaming in each installation. "This is the next wave of nanotechnology. Art that's alive. Only a few, like you, can hear as we do. Feel as we do. Join us."

Penny looks around the garden. The creations are beautiful, waving in the wind. As if they are waving to Penny. A tickle begins in her brain as Oliver waves his hands at the Kutulu, summoning his nano-material.

She sways with the spires. Excitement crackles in her veins and Penny is hungry. For fish, for human flesh, for the promise of violence. Her eyes fall on Oliver's hands. It looks like radioactive gum is stuck under his fingernails.

She does a quick jumping jack to refocus herself. "Your hands, how does that goo--"

"Goo? Are you that uncultured?" Oliver grits his teeth, his voice cracking, then catches himself.

Penny's eyes widen, the brain tickle gone. She feels restless, exhausted and a bit irritable. A flash of memory, this is a similar low after the cocaine high.

"Where did fighting get you in the past?" He opens his arms. "I can see that you have grit, you don't give up. We need your energy. Join us. Aren't you tired of being alone?"

A force is caressing her brain, promising another high, another hit. Penny bites her lip and concentrates on Oliver, not letting the addictive red swim across her brain again.

"I'm alone, but my brain is also my own." Penny grimaces. "What is the Kutulu? What would I be joining?"

"The Kutulu are undefinable. A new world order. Open your mind, I will show you."

Penny digs her nails into her palms, keeping the tingle at the edge of her cerebral cortex. "How will this help humanity?"

Oliver gestures at his latest Kutulu. The multi-colored tentacles reaching for the sun. "Instead of billions of people going different directions, we are a hive-mind. Nano-bytes and energy working together."

"Working towards what?" She reaches a hand towards the swaying Kutulu.

"The next wave of evolution." Oliver steps closer. "Take the leap of faith, Penny, like I did."

His voice massages her brain. The tingle creeps in. She hardly notices when he touches her lip.

"How Oliver?" Her voice sounds slurred. "How did you leap?"

"I was a professor working with biomedical nanotechnology. Art was just my hobby. It was a lucky accident; I added a bit of meteorite from the school's geology museum to my nanotubes!"

Oliver edges closer to her. "But they had no vision. I was fired instead."

"Like you tried to fire me?" Penny struggles to move, but she's frozen.

Oliver runs his finger along the edge of her mouth.

The Kutulu sway in the botanical garden, their long arms

unfurling and knocking flowers off of cacti. Penny's mind hums with them.

"How do you get from nanotubes, to being fired, to creating living art from your fingers?" She holds his hand still on her mouth.

"I ate some of my research." A bit of orange liquid spills onto her bottom lip from his finger.

It's warm and Penny parts her lips. It will feel so good to belong. To be a part of something, all that energy...

Over her boss's shoulder, she sees a 900-year-old Saguaro cactus fall to the ground. The once impressive plant is shrunken and dehydrated. The yellow Kutulu beside it twists its tendrils, swelling with growth. Penny knocks Oliver's hand away and spits the bit of orange fluid off her lip. A tiny pebble bounces on the ground.

"You're insane."

Penny judges the distance between her and the dropped saw. With a shake of her head, she clears the call of the Kutulu, the urge to feel that red high vanquished.

Oliver's pupils dilate when he senses she is no longer connected to the hive mind.

"You had your chance to be one with us. Now you will be eaten. The gristle and bone are needed for us to grow."

The multi-colored Kutulu unfurls and reaches for her. A gaping mouth at the end of each tube.

Penny jumps, hitting the ground and rolling. She makes a swipe at her saw. Her hand narrowly misses it.

The red arm of the Kutulu grabs her shirt and sucks it off her back. She shrieks and runs, feeling the tendril tips brush her skin. It's like a vacuum cleaner has latched onto her calves. Some of her hair gets caught and her ball cap gets torn off her head. Yanking her ponytail out of a black tube, and kicking off a pink one, she runs. Runs like shrapnel is propelling her. Runs for her life.

Once she is past the Koi Pond, she feels safer. The Kutulu can stretch their curly bits, but the trunks are embedded in the earth. Or in the case of the pond Kutulu, in the water. Even though she is out of reach, Penny doesn't slow, heading for the gardening shed.

"The world is a mess; you know this better than anyone. Come back!" Oliver picks up the saw and follows.

Penny strains her legs and pumps her arms. Out of the corner of her eye she can see her boss rounding the pond. His belly jiggles as he scuttles. His coke-bottle glasses are askew and he's brandishing the saw like a sword. Diving into the shed, Penny slams the door behind her and blocks it with the industrial lawn mower.

A fist pounds on the old wood, "Penny, you can still join us. Don't be the Dodo. Evolve!"

"I thought you said I was gristle. Make up your mind, Oliver." Penny picks up a bag of fertilizer.

"We don't want to hurt you." Oliver uses the tip of the saw and stabs through the door.

Grabbing the jerry can of fuel, she tries to crack open the single window. The saw has sheared a hole in the door now and Oliver's red face peers in. She grunts, pushing on the window. It's glued shut with paint.

"Right, you and your Kutulu come in peace?" Penny shoves the fertilizer bag through the window. The shatter and clinking of the glass drowning out Oliver.

"--eaten, or do the eating." He busts through his jagged hole, swearing as he stumbles over the lawnmower.

Penny checks the lid on the jerry can and throws it after the fertilizer. Then she grabs the jagged edge of the broken window, wincing as the glass cuts her palms--

Oliver is so close; she can feel his hot breath. The saw slams into her ankle and blood gushes into her shoe.

--she flings herself out the window, somersaulting into the grass. Wiping her palms on her shorts, she can see the cuts are deep. Her ankle is seeping blood from an inch-wide cut. Limping as fast as she can, she carries the fertilizer and the can of fuel back to the Kutulu. The multi-colored one is stretching shiny opaque tubes, trying to catch her hair or a bit of skin.

Keeping a wide berth, Penny would love to blow up the biggest Kutulu, but the water is a problem. She skirts the edge of the pond and makes a quick dash at the Yellow Kutulu. The one that ate her hummingbird. Before it can unfurl its spirals, she rips open the fertilizer bag.

"No." Oliver falls to his knees on the other side of the pond.

She opens the jerry can and glugs fuel on the mix. A yellow arm swipes at her, giving her ear a good zing. Before it can attach, she skuttles on her hands and knees out of reach.

She waits for the explosion, hands on her ears.

Nothing.

She whacks her forehead with one bloody palm.

"Of course, I need a catalyst," she says under her breath.

"Penny, what's waiting for you at home? Bad memories and Merlot?" Oliver's palms are pressed together, praying.

She furls her eyebrows. "I need a stick of dynamite. A blasting cap."

"You need peace, you need to become one of us," Oliver says.

Penny's limbs are trembling from blood loss, exhaustion. "I do need peace."

"Help me with opening day tomorrow. It will be so beautiful, crowds of energy-filled people, the sky lit up with fireworks. Be a part of history."

The Kutulu are waving in the warm breeze, moving with the cadence of Oliver's voice. Penny feels herself swaying with them. The sun reflects off their iridescent arms. She closes her eyes against the brightness.

She feels drunk, compliant. "Opening day tomorrow. I will be a part of history. We will celebrate with fireworks."

The fireworks. Her eyes fly open.

Duty before Death.

She squeezes her nails into her hands, firing up the wound to wake herself up. She gasps and charges towards the supervisor tent. It's only a few feet from the yellow Kutulu. From Oliver's trolley, she picks out an M-80, the most powerful kind of firework. It has a label on it. 'Grand Finale.'

"Don't do it." Oliver gasps.

She pulls out her baggie with her one cigarette and takes out the box of matches and ignites the M-80. It sparks and flares. She flings it at the fertilizer fuel pile at the base of the Kutulu.

Oliver's enormous eyes bulge.

She runs, like she did in Afghanistan, back to her Humvee.

The ground heaves and booms pierce the air. The gardening shed goes up. A bigger boom. Shattering metal. Flying tiles. Spiny green bits of cacti. Multi-colored shards of Kutulu. Half a pair of coke-bottle glasses.

Penny is lifted into the air, her arms pinwheeling. She is catapulted behind her truck. Her ears ring while sharp pieces of debris pelt her back. Everything goes black.

HER EYES flicker open and her body hurts. Her hands, her back, her ankle, her head. Grimacing she tests out her body parts. She is sticky with blood but everything seems to be in working order. No broken bones. She climbs onto the hood of her Humvee. With her hands on her hips, she surveys the aftermath.

Smoke is rising from where the Kutulu used to stand. Little balls of every color are sizzling on the ground.

"Oliver?"

No answer. No sign of him.

The beautiful gardens are destroyed but the devastation is only about a mile wide. Outside of the blast zone, the tall Saguaro tower in the distance. The sheer cliffs of Spur Cross Conservation Area on the horizon.

A smile pulls at her lips and she lights her one cigarette. The smoke mingles with the vapor from the nano-monsters. A coyote edges onto the blackened sand and looks at her curiously.

"Yup. Penny saves the day. Guess this old soldier still has a bit of fight left in her." She nods to the grey animal.

He sniffs at a purple ball.

"You better leave that, puppy." Penny flicks her cigarette at the coyote.

The coyote spooks at the stub, but before he can run away, the purple bit of Kutulu rolls onto his paw and quickly spreads up his leg. He yelps and a purple tendril grows out of its ear. He whines as the goo digs itself into the earth and coats his entire body. A miniature Kutulu forms, little spirals unfurling and reaching for the sky.

"No, no, no no." Penny jumps off the hood and falls to her knees on the black earth.

A bunny rabbit sniffs at a yellow ball and screams as it is slowly encased. The furry body becomes a trunk and a yellow Kutulu joins the purple. Baby saplings of horror. She squints at the destruction caused by her bomb. Red, blue, yellow, purple, and orange balls everywhere.

"What have I done?"

The wind blows a yellow ball of glowing matter next to her leg. Penny picks it up and looks at it, biting her lower lip. As she holds it the light dims and the color seeps from the little sphere. Rolling it in her palm, it feels dead. No tingle, no warmth. A hummingbird pauses in front of her, little wings a flurry.

"Would you look at that? The Kutulu particles are strong together, but lose all power divided."

She lifts a hand to her forehead and surveys the horizon. A few new Kutulu are growing, but most of the balls are dead and grey. The hummingbird flits towards the small yellow Kutulu.

"Stay away little one." Penny cautions.

With a juicy slurp the yellow Kutulu sucks up the bird and grows a little taller. The purple Kutulu shudders. She can feel the tingle at the edge of her brain as they hum.

Penny heads to her Humvee and pulls a Glock 42 pistol out of her glove box. The one she was keeping as a last resort. Her exit plan. Gripping it in her palm, she stalks back to the two baby Kutulu.

"Hooah, nano-assholes." Penny pulls the trigger.

The bullets tear into the structures and shatter them. Wincing, she feels a stabbing in her cerebral cortex, but it fades as she keeps pulling the trigger. Purple and yellow balls fly onto the desert sand, gleam brightly for a moment, and then fade to grey.

Penny climbs back into the Humvee and reloads her gun. In the distance she sees several new Kutulu glistening and stretching for the sky. Given life by an unfortunate coyote, bunny, or other passing animal before the balls lost their power. Closing her eyes to concentrate, she can feel the slight tingling. The mini Kutulu are calling to her. A huge grin splits her face. She has purpose now.

"Penny the Kutulu Killer. It has a nice ring to it." She puts the Humvee into gear and drives out into the desert. "Let the hunt begin."

3

___

ABOUT "DEATH METAL FAN"

~

First published: April 2019
Hawntedmtl.com

THIS STORY GOES *to some very dark places. What would you do if a room fan sang evil suggestions? Follow them of course.*

4

DEATH METAL FAN

BY ANGELIQUE FAWNS

The weather was unbearably hot. Smoking, steaming, bra-dripping hot. Mia lay on top of her bed with a fan blowing air on her body. Moderate relief.

It was Canada Day and the firecrackers were ringing and lighting up the sky outside her window even though it was almost midnight. Mia had foregone any celebrations this year. She couldn't imagine facing 43-degree weather, plus bugs for hours just to watch different colours light up the sky. Whoop dee doo.

That's not all she couldn't face. Her boyfriend dumped her a week ago. The married boyfriend who was going to leave his wife for her. She'd hung in for five years… letting her late twenties and early thirties pass her by. Her friends told her she was being dumb. And she was. Another cliché. Another woman who thought they actually had something real. His wife wasn't kind to him. They were married in name only. Yadda yadda yadda. Ya right.

She didn't need to see the 'I told you so' expressions on her friends' faces. Or hear the saccharine empathy. It was all too nauseating. Her self-loathing was suffocating her. She'd always been able to catch the eyes of men with her long curly black hair and Kardashian curves, but the years were catching up to her. A few less construction workers were whistling at her. Less eyes turning at the local bars. So, she lay here wallowing in her sweat. Alone. Wondering if she could actually melt into a congealed lump on her bedspread. That would be the way to go. Mia missing. Slime ball found.

Feeling her eyelids succumb to slime state Mia fell asleep.

Until she was woken up by someone playing loud Death Metal. Her alarm clock read 3:00am in digital red. Who was having a Canada Day party this late? And who even listened to Death Metal anymore? Wasn't that an 80's thing?

She could hear the lead vocalist growling out "Give me a quuuuuuuuuuuuu. Give me a yooooooooou. Give me an eeeeeeye . Give me an ellllllllllllllllll. And an ellllllllllll. And a sssssssssss."

Being a fan of both country <u>and </u>western music, but not much else, she had no idea what band was playing. The lead singer sounded like Glenn Danzig from the Misfits after inhaling live flame. Here came the chorus again.

"Give me a quuuuuuuuuuuuu. Give me a yooooooooou. Give me an eeeeeeye . Give me an ellllllllllllllllll. And an ellllllllllll. And a sssssssssss."

Give me Quills? What an odd song lyric. This was ridiculous, how was she supposed to sleep? And didn't her neighbours go away camping this weekend so who was home blaring music? The properties in this neighbourhood weren't that close together, and she was sure the retired octogenarians on the other side of her weren't rocking out.

Mia unstuck her body from the sheets and crawled to the end of the bed to shut off the fan. It was stationed in front of the window to pull in the cool air. (What cool air?) She wanted to hear where the music was coming from. Turning off the fan she listened closely... and heard nothing.

How odd. Did they just turn the music off? She couldn't hear anything. No talking, no laughing. No music. Nothing. Mia was stumped. She turned the fan back on and slithered back up to her pillows. She tried to find a dry spot. Laying there, she heard it again.

"Give me a quuuuuuuuu....."

Holy crap. Was it coming from the fan? Mia quickly moved down to the fan and turned it off. No singer. She turned it on.

"Give me a youuuuuuuuu"

Good god. Her fan was singing Death Metal at her. Spelling the word Quills. If possible, she started to sweat more and felt her heart racing. She decided this was something she didn't want to ponder too deeply in the middle of the night. It was far too hot to turn the fan off, so she let the raspy voice lull her back to sleep.

In the morning, Mia woke up and listened to her fan. It was just a fan. Making a whiiiiirr sound.

Mia worked as fourth grade teacher at a public school in Richmond Hill and had the next two months off. Yaaaay. Her class had been full of nasty little girls being as mean to each other as only 8-year-olds could be. She had to deal with so many tears, she feels like she absorbed any misery her Kleenex missed. These two months would be a perfect time to recuperate. From the pre-teen drama and her own drama. But Quills. Why Quills?

Time to consult Google. The first and most obvious hit was that super creepy movie in 2000 about the Marquis de Sade. Mia remembered watching it and feeling like she lost any innocence she had left. The sadism and masochism, the blood, and all the other bodily fluids that sick man played with. Yuck. Next was an on-line writing course for young students. Then she saw a listing for a bookstore near her. Just in Aurora, not a twenty-minute walk away. Maybe this was the Quills her fan was moaning about?

Coincidence? She had nothing else doing that day, so she swept her brown curly hair into a messy bun, threw on some jean shorts, a red I AM CANADIAN t-shirt and started hiking to Quills "the bookstore". The Greater Toronto area was still under a heat warning, so it felt like walking through soup. In April snow was still coating the ground, so she reminded herself to enjoy not being frozen to death and let the exercise perk her up.

It was a small shop with windows obscured by books piled up haphazardly on the sills. The front door was covered with pamphlets, post-its and advertisements for local events. Concert listings for bands with charming names like Death, Cannibal Corpse and Morbid Angel. Everything looked like it had been there for 20 years except for the shiny black sign "Quills" above the door. Mia pushed the door in and a set of bells announced her arrival.

Inside books were jammed on shelves, piled on the floor and stacked on tables everywhere. Most of the books appeared to be used, and that peculiar musty smell from damp paper was in the air. Science fiction, horror, and teen trilogies seemed to rule the genres. She saw lots of Isaac Asimov anthologies, Stephen King, Dean Koontz, and Twilight series books in her first perusal of the stacks.

"Ummm. Can I help you?" A nasally voice asked.

Mia looked around and sees a man with pock-marked cheeks and hair sticking straight up on his head behind the register. The counter had so many books on it she hadn't even seen him when she came in.

"Just looking," Mia said.

"What do you need? I can make recommendations, I just got some James Patterson books in, some Suzanne Collins if you like the Hunger Games," he emerged from his book barricade and Mia saw he was tall and painfully thin. His Adams apple protruded and bobbed as he spoke.

"Why Quills? How did you come up with the name for this place?" She asked while running her hands along the spines of the books on the closest shelf.

"It used to be Pete's Place, my older brother's store. But he lived life on-the-edge. Live by the sword, die by the sword they say. Ha. So, I took it over. But my name's not Pete and I didn't think Irwin's Place sounded that great, ha-ha. My favorite movie is Quills, and books used to be written with Quills, so Quills it became," Irwin said as his nervous giggle trailed off.

"What happened to your brother?" Mia asked, hoping her sweat wasn't sticking her t-shirt to her boobs in a grossly sexy way. She could see Irwin talking more to her chest than her face.

"He was murdered a few months ago. A robbery gone wrong they say. But this place makes no money, so it never made sense to me. Ha-ha. Pete ran with a rough crowd, so I told the cops to check out his party buds, but they couldn't figure out who killed him. Wish we had cameras, he was killed right here. But no money, no cameras. Ha-ha," Irwin's twitchy laugh getting worse the more he talked. His eyes were now travelling the whole length of her body.

"Well I am so sorry for your loss," Mia said as she turned to leave the store.

There was no air conditioning and just one big ground fan stirring the pages of the books lucky enough to be in front of it. She was hot, uncomfortable, and horrified. The owner of this store was recently murdered? And she was sent here by her fan? She obviously needed to book a therapy session or ten.

She walked out into the even warmer street and was about to walk home when WHAM. A cyclist got creamed at the intersection. The truck turning left didn't see the man peddling across the road. Blood spray everywhere, and cars honked and screeched to a stop. The violence of the moment electrified the air. Mia felt adrenaline rush through her system. Her nipples got hard and a warm tingling started in her shorts. Instead of joining the chaos of bystanders rushing to assist, she turned and went back into the store.

Irwin was back behind his book wall.

"What was that? Was someone hit at that terrible intersection again? Happens all the time," he said no giggle in his voice now.

"Yes. Is there a place we can go?" Mia said, pushing out the boobs she was trying to hide before.

"What?" Irwin gaped at her in confusion, actually bringing his eyes up to her face.

"A place we can be alone." Mia gave him a slow wink.

Rather than answer he rushed to the front door and flipped the sign to "Closed".

"Umm, haha, right back here," he said, his voice going up a few octaves and cracking in excitement.

Irwin led her into a back-storage room, and as soon as he closed the door, Mia took off her shorts and t-shirt.

"Okay, Mr. Hot Bookstore owner, show me what you're hiding

under those shorts." Mia cringed at her own bad dialogue. Lord, she was going to have to get some better seduction lines.

Irwin almost tripped himself trying to get out of his clothes. Mia's pretty sure this scenario has never happened to him before.

Then she rode him. She used him. The thought of that blood, of the carnage outside, she can't believe how excited it made her. She bossed him around. It's was the most amazing fifteen minutes ever. Random sex with a distinctly unhot dude? Completely out of character for her. When they're done, they're both coated in a sticky sweat. Mia threw her clothes on and went back into the main book store area without even looking at Irwin. She stood in front of the big fan and let the cool air blow down her shirt.

Irwin followed her, pulling his t-shirt on backwards. "Uh, that was great. Can I get your number?"

"Don't talk. Don't ruin it," Mia said as she pulled her shirt and bra out to let more air from the store fan cool her skin. Irwin went back behind the counter but peeked out at her from behind the entire Twilight series by Stephanie Myers.

Then she heard it. Glenn Danzig but darker.

"Give me an rrrrrrrrrrrrrr. Give me an eeeeeeeeeeee. Give me a beeeeeeee. Give me an eeeeeeeee. Give me an ellllllllll."

Mia leant into the fan and heard it again. The faint growly voice singing out letters.

"Rebel," she whispered to herself. She doesn't have to Google this one. Rebel is the hottest nightclub in Toronto and it's right down by the lake. Without a backwards glance at goggle-eyed Irwin she walked out of Quills and headed back home. The poor cyclist was just getting loaded into an ambulance, but Mia wasn't interested anymore. She's planning her outfit for tonight. Time to go dancing.

Normally Mia's wardrobe is conservative. Knee length skirts. Modest necklines. But she felt like a new Mia. The kind of Mia who rocks a twenty-year-old geek's world and takes what she wants. This kind of lady wears a tight black dress. Short. Low neckline. She dug through her closet until she found some dusty dresses from her university days. Yes. She found one suitably sexy for a night at Rebel. With a bit of Spanx, this dress could still turn some heads.

She contemplated calling one of her friends to come with her, but they might not know what to make of this new Mia. She doesn't want to lose this bold adventure-y feeling she has inside. They'll think she's on aself-destructive rebound kick. (Is she?) She's no longer the scorned woman left by her married lover. She's a lady who's gone absolutely bat-shit crazy listening to messages sent to her by floor fans. She's getting turned on by bloody accidents and having sex with strangers. Later she'll call a therapist. Sign up for maybe fifteen sessions.

At around 9:00pm she left her bungalow and drove down to Toronto's Harbourfront. Finding rock-star parking on Polson Street, she strutted into Rebel's cavernous converted warehouse. Psychedelic strobe lights illuminated the dance floor and bodies gyrated to music spun by DJ Deadmau5.

Not sure what she was looking for and seeing no available fans ready to give instructions, Mia headed up to the mezzanine. After buying a watered-down gin and tonic for $8.50. (Good lord this place is expensive!) She sat down on a couch near a group of flashy club goers.

"So, there's lots of Blue Dolphin here, but how do I get myself some Purple Pete?" an Italian guy in a custom suit asked a blonde woman in a sequined tea towel on the couch behind her.

"It used to be you could only get Purple Pete from this place in Aurora. A hole in the wall bookstore called Pete's Place. But it was the best ecstasy on the market. Rumor has it he made it right on premises. But now Damon is holding some," the blonde said while wiggling on her seat trying to make sure the tea towel kept her strategic parts covered.

"Is Damon here tonight?" asked the Italian guy looking around and gulping at his Heineken

"Damon is always here," the blonde answered and nodded in the direction of a tall man wearing jeans and a sport jacket leaning on the mezzanine railing. The second floor of the club had a low glass wall encircling it so guests could lean over and stare at the writhing bodies below.

Mia watched as Italian guy walked over and spent a few minutes talking to Damon. The transaction was over quickly, and the couch behind her emptied out to go down to the dance floor. The second floor was basically deserted. Mia tossed her hair over one eye, hiked up her skirt and walked over to Damon.

"Purple Pete please," she said in her sexiest voice.

"Thirty bucks a pill," Damon said and ran his predatory eyes up and down Mia's body. "This stuff makes you want to party. I'd wouldn't mind partying alone with you later."

Mia flicked out her tongue at him and sidled closer. (She's rusty, so she's hoping tongue flicking is sexy.)

"Lean back and maybe we can do some partying now. It's dark and there's no one up here" she purred while rotating her hips in a suggestive way and doing another tongue flick.

Damon put his hands on his hips and leaned back on the railing as Mia knelt down in front of him.

"Oh ya, consider your first pill comped." Damon said as he zipped down his pants.

Rather than drop to her knees, Mia tucked one shoulder forward, thrust up on her legs, and heaved him over the railing.

If Damon screamed on the way down to the dance floor, she couldn't hear it. Mia's blood pumped quickly through her veins and a delightful shot of serotonin lit up her brain. Wow. What a rush. Forget Purple Pete, she'd take the Red Damon please. Red bloody Damon she thought with joy. Looking around, no one seemed to have noticed anything on the mezzanine. She walked quickly towards the bathrooms and back stairs away from the main floor overlook. What was going on with her? She felt like she did after riding Irwin. Powerful. Sated. Aroused. No amount of therapy was going to save her now.

As she climbed down the back stairs, the music stopped and the regular lights came back on. She could hear the shocked gasps and screams coming from the dance floor. She walked back towards the front of the club and joined the crowd around the sprawled man.

God, it was like art, the way the blood was splattered around his body.

"What happened?" she asked a couple beside her, making sure no saw that he was pushed.

The girl sobbed, "a guy fell over the wall and he's dead!"

Her date said, "this is going to ruin the party tonight."

Mia thanked them and headed rapidly for the door. She's got to get out before they decide to shut the place down and have cops interview everyone. A few other clubbers had the same idea and they all walked out of the front door together in the chaos and confusion.

Driving home, Mia held onto the tingly unfamiliar feeling in her stomach. She felt free, happy, corrupt and like a totally new person. Did she just avenge Pete's death? Was he the voice in her fan? That was pretty crazy to contemplate but strange things happened everyday.

When she got home she ripped off her black dress and hopped naked into bed. Even though the night is cooler, she makes sure her fan is going full tilt. And she listens......

5

ABOUT "INK"

~

First published: September 2022
Maul Magazine

AKIS LINARDOS IS a guest author in this collection, and he tells a terrifying tale of an ink splotch with an ulterior motive.

IN A COVE OF A GREEK ISLAND, Akis was born a sane infant, but has since then grown to enter the chaotic world of adults--a choice he deeply regrets. His stories delve both into epic worlds and ones of extreme darkness. Find him at Apex, Dread Machine, Flame Tree and numerous anthologies. https://linktr.ee/akislinardos

6

___

INK

BY AKIS LINARDOS

It started as a moldy splotch on one corner of the living room ceiling, soon expanding into a long crescent like the smile of a goddamn Cheshire cat. I squeeze a mop on it and rub until my muscles ache behind my elbows. The mop gets black and smudgy, and it smells funny. Like fresh concrete.

I call the handyman. He says he'll come tomorrow.

As I hang up, I hear the elevator mid-whirr outside my apartment. It only goes as high as this, though there is one extra floor above, accessible only by stairs. Where Oswald lives.

I see him from the eyehole. He's carrying a massive oil barrel— black paint for his art, I assume. He's dragging the barrel up the spiral stairs, struggling to twist it around the tight corners. Perhaps he needs help?

I grab the handle, pause.

Why should I help him? He never bothers with my problems. Barely even talks to me these days.

I push the door open anyway. "Do you need help, Oswald?"

"Ah, no bother. I've got it," he says, barely glancing in my direction. When had I become invisible to him?

"What's that you've got over there?" I ask.

His mouth curls into a smirk. "Just some supplies."

"I did some painting the other day after a long time. It kinda flowed out of me. Maybe you can take a look sometime."

"That's nice," he says.

He doesn't even hear me. Doesn't even look at me. The message in his eyes and in his tone is clear: *Why is that loser still talking to me?*

The genius polymath, an archeologist with a passion for cartoons —successful in both. Ever since he uncovered that jar from the buried ziggurat in Peru, he'd been the buzz of the town. Who has time to even glance at his childhood friend with all the media attention and busy life, right? Who has time to waste on a loser?

Whatever. I don't care.

"Well, enjoy," I say, and retreat to my apartment.

I lay on the couch and stare at the ceiling. A screech moves along it, and I imagine something sharp and heavy slowly being dragged against the floor above. My brain hurts, like cold spoons slowly being dragged beneath my temples. The Cheshire smile curls wider on the ceiling.

THE HANDYMAN CRAWLS through the scuttle attic between my room and Oswald's. The scuttle hole releases a wave of stench, like someone had tossed rotten fruit into a bowlful of wet cement. I feel sorry for the handyman.

I sit back on the coffee-stained couch and turn on the TV. Show's about to start: Oswald's Fermi the Bouncy Rat. The show that brought black-and-white cartoons back in fashion. I'll never understand how Oswald managed it. He followed his dreams all the way to Wonderland. Not that I'm jealous of him. The pharmacy pays the bills, so I never stress about money. I'm happy with my life.

The handyman crawls back out an hour later. Says he couldn't find any leaks from the boiler, and that whatever the hell it was, it's all over the scuttle, but it's even worse above. Must be something from upstairs. I have to figure it out with Oswald.

So I'll be the one speaking to him again. Begging for his attention.

I can't remember when we stopped being friends. It happened like a slow shifting of seasons: from best friends, to occasional updates on each other's life, to a polite greeting in the common areas. Reduced to stranger neighbors.

He usually comes home around five thirty. I'll have to think about how to phrase my request casually. I hate needy people. I don't want to give that impression.

I spend some time at the coffee table with the TV on, working on a cartoon rabbit sketch I started some six months ago and never got to finish. Not much of a point to it, the lines come out all awkward again. The eyes don't match.

I remember the first time my father found me painting. *"Good hobby, keeps the eye sharp. But don't do it for a living. Pharmacy will set you up for life. People always need their pills."* He never really understood. Not like Oswald's parents did. They paid his tuition through art school, talked up his paintings every chance they'd get. It's different if you have someone cheering you on. But he was lucky. I was not. Simple as that.

The elevator whirrs. The familiar jingle of Oswald's bulky keyring follows.

I reach the door, wrap my fingers around the cold handle, stay there for a long moment. All the opening phrases I stored up seem clunky and awkward.

His footsteps taper away, up the stairs. I push the door open. He's halfway up the staircase, hand on the railings.

"Hey, Oswald. I'll need your help one of these days. Something wrong with the ceiling. Found out yesterday the problem comes from your place."

He turns. Slowly. Precisely. Like a goddamn clockwork soldier.

There's something along his neck. A dark scar or a tattoo half-hidden by his collar. Reminds me of a black snake's tail. That's new. He looks at me for a long while with glazed, distant eyes. Then says,

"Want to hear what I found out yesterday? A scripture from the jar of Acat." His voice gets lower. "*Taste the ink. Scar yourself with the mark of gods.*"

Is he making fun of me? "I don't speak whatever language it is you're speaking. There's something wrong with the ceiling. It's full of mold, and the problem comes from your place. Could you bring a handyman to figure it out? It's a mess on my side."

"Mayans had such fascinating gods. They'd paint themselves in Acat's name. They were His canvas."

I don't care. "Right, good job, Oswald. Well, I'll be around if you need someone to talk to about it. But please call a handyman."

"Mayans would put a plank on the newborns' foreheads," Oswald continued. "Press it tight with a bandage and leave it there to elongate their skulls as they grow. Acat had more room to paint that way. I also found that out yesterday. Or maybe a week ago. Time slips lately."

What the hell is his problem? Does he want to make me mad? "That's interesting. Please take care of this mold issue, though. I can call him for you if you prefer."

He smiles, and the smile reminds me of the Oswald I used to know as a kid. When he'd run so fast I couldn't catch up, and he'd turn around with a grin to tell me how amazingly bad I was at every-thing. "I'll take care of it, man. Don't worry about it."

THE MIGRAINES ARE GETTING WORSE. My skull bones have been wobbling like cymbals all day today, and I snapped at an old lady at the pharmacy. Good customer, too. Pretty sure I lost her forever. I toss out my shoes as I walk into my apartment, rub my temples as I trudge to the kitchen for tea. I avoid looking at the ceiling. It's been four days, and I haven't heard back from Oswald. He is so busy with his precious work I doubt he remembers what I asked him to do.

When I saw him the other day, he didn't even acknowledge my presence. Something off with him too, mouth all grimy with some-thing dark. Looked like a kid that had gotten into the chocolate box. Perhaps adulthood won't allow him time to wipe his arse, either.

I take the tea to the living room, smell the jasmine to calm my nerves, never looking up, never looking at the half-finished sketch on the coffee table. Too tired to finish it today.

A random thought strikes me. I whip out my phone and look up the words *Taste the ink. Mark yourself with the scar of gods.* Or was it scar first, mark second? Neither gives me any result. What was that god's name? Acat. I look that up.

No wonder Oswald comes up with creepy cartoons if he's into that stuff. What he said the other day is true. Mayans were deforming their own babies. The richer they were, the more grotesque the deformation to stand out. Blood offerings. Human sacrifice. It was all viewed as nourishment for the gods. Gods cannot take a life. They can only devour a freshly killed soul.

A droplet spills into my tea from above, suffusing the clear yellow with black. I look up.

Lumps of the black mold have bloated out of the ceiling. They remind me of wasp nests. I'll give that bastard a good yelling tomorrow. Too tired now. I fall asleep on the couch, Fermi the Bouncy Rat playing on the TV screen. I like the noise. I can't sleep in the quiet. Fermi's cartoon-spring sounds soothe me, and I drift asleep feeling a tickle in my left ear. Like a tiny tongue.

It's some alien hour past midnight when I awake with a rank, oily taste in the back of my throat. Something skitters down my arm and away with bouncy sounds. *Boing, boing, boing.* The sounds vanish toward the exit. My left ear feels cold. I touch it. Wet with something slimy. I turn the lamp on.

My arm is covered in tiny spots, as if a cockroach stepped on black paint before having a stroll from my wrist to my elbow. Black splotches all over the floor. One on the TV screen. And there's a crack on the glass nearly as big as my fist, the shards spread out on the floor in front.

A migraine hits. My forehead burns. I tilt my head back. Above, the wasp blobs of mold seem to be pulsating.

I call Oswald. The phone rings back a Vivaldi season I cannot place—though it's not Winter. My throat feels parched. I smack my lips and eye the cup on my coffee table. Idly, I take a sip of the cold tea. Tastes sweet as honey, though I don't recall adding any sugar. Oswald doesn't respond. My brain throbs. I swear it's trying to escape my damn skull.

Screw this.

The black splotches lead out of my apartment, upstairs, to Oswald's place. With every dazed step up the stairs, my eyes seem to wobble in their sockets, burning all over. His door is ajar. A thick musky haze permeates from within like blackened shower vapors. It smells like carbonized soot and feels like grease on my skin as I enter the living room.

Have I walked into a dream? Or was I trapped in a cycle of dreams for weeks now, in a comatose state, unable to wake up?

"Oswald? Oswald, what—" I taste coal and shut my mouth, letting out a burst of muffled coughs.

It's a meandering corridor to reach the living room. Something punctures my foot, and I let out a yelp. I pull my sock off, cursing, and squeeze out a splinter of wood and a sanguine little marble from the toe. As I rub the rough outline of the skin, I capture oily black snowflakes between finger and toe and spread smudge on both.

I cup my mouth with both hands and yell again.

"Oswald, man, what the hell? Didn't you hear me scream? My ceiling looks like a Jackson Pollock of mold and it won't go away."

I step into the living room.

"What have you been—"

His body is surrounded by lit candles. Tattoos have spread to his face in a spiderweb. His eyes are egg-whites lying in charcoal-mud skin. The black liquid slowly spreads inside the eyes.

A prank. He'll jump-scare me now, jolt awake and shift his eyes. Oswald was always up to mischief as a child.

Only we weren't children anymore.

His chest still heaves. He is breathing. The Jar of Acat is beside him, overfull with the black liquid of art. The ink surface balloons in and out of the jar in pulses, as if it's also breathing.

The tattoos shift on Oswald's body. On his belly, a black dog takes shape, chasing a black cat as a squiggly line beneath them undulates to give the illusion of movement in space. The cat pulls out a hammer, smashes the dog's head, laughs in a goofy gurgle.

On Oswald's face, black stripes curve to spirals, merge, stretch out to two curved lines that form between them the outlines of buck teeth. The sketched mouth opens. A low husky voice comes from it, maybe of some creature suffering from pneumonia.

"Taste the ink. Scar yourself with the mark of gods."

"What...?"

The mouth bulges out, a black balloon at Oswald's cheek. Buck teeth, pointy ears, pacman-shaped irises. It bounces off him. It's Fermi, the Bouncy Rat.

"You want it," it says as it springs from Oswald's solar plexus, as it bounces off walls, spreading the ink. *"You want the blessings others have. Why should others have all the luck, while your dreams are slowly dying? He did it, why not you? Taste the ink. Then sacrifice him."*

The splotches the rat leaves on the walls spread out in a spider-web, forming the shapes I recognize from Oswald's cartoons. Centie the Zebra Centipede skitters up to the ceiling, its tiny bowlegs clacking like notes on a marimba. Is this the source of Oswald's success? Has he stumbled upon a hidden occult treasure that somehow fell through the cracks of human history?

I know I should be afraid, but I'm not. My chest pounds with excitement. Whatever happens next, how can it be worse than the listlessness of my mundane one-bedroom-apartment life filled with taxes and pills and cranky old ladies and rusted dreams?

"What are you? What did you do to him?"

The cartoons twist on the walls. The cat from before walks up the stairs of a ziggurat. Its head elongates. Longer with every step. And as its head grows, diamond rings materialize around its loony feline hands, dark blood spills from its mouth. The cat reaches the top, lets out another goofy gurgle. Its head explodes in a splash of ink.

"You're Acat," I say.

The creature does not respond.

I inhale deeply, taking in the oily scent, tasting charcoal and honey beneath my tongue. My heart drums with every *boing* of that rat, with every gurgle laughter and xylophone skittering of the cartoons on the walls. It's like they spring against my cranium. Crawl along my spine. And here's the strangest thing: I enjoy it. The migraine is gone, transformed into a pleasant stupor of intoxication. Like those nights pub crawling around town and having just the right amount to drink. Not too much, certainly not too little. A ticket straight to Wonderland.

Oswald lies in a pool of his own avarice, ink mingled with bubbling saliva spilling out of his mouth. He failed. He was the real loser all along. My mouth curls into a grin, and my mirth comes bursting out in a cackle. For the first time in years, I feel alive.

I grab the knife, dip it into the jar, then out. Delicious molten tar drips from the blade. I will never end up like him. I'll make that goddamn Wonderland mine, baby.

I bring the blade's spine close to my mouth, and lick.

7

———

ABOUT "THE GOLDEN FALCON"

~

First published: October 2020
Coffin Blossoms

THIS STORY TAKES a trope and flips it upside down. What if a cursed trailer made its inhabitants more intelligent? A comedy horror romance with a twist.

8

THE GOLDEN FALCON

BY ANGELIQUE FAWNS

*T*here is nothing more satisfying than taking a shower in someone else's bathroom. Especially when the owners don't know you're enjoying their Body Spa Shower System, natural stone flooring, and unlimited hot water. Two hipsters, Suzette and Fergus, owned this McMansion on the good side of Mud Lake and worked in the city. I walked their Labradoodle Django for them every weekday.

I lived with my ma in her Winnebago on the other side of the lake. Her plumbing was rusty and the water hardly worked in the tiny lav. I'd left Django in the backyard with a piece of deer antler, so he wouldn't whine and bug me. Stepping out of the enormous glass stall, I wrapped myself in the little beach towel I brought and would take with me. No evidence.

I'd left my leopard print onesie in the master bedroom, and was toweling off my hair walking down the hall, when I saw a tall man with a rat-tail mullet leaning over the dresser and sorting through Suzette's jewelry. I screamed and tried to cover myself with the little towel. He whirled and pointed a BB gun at me.

"Whoa put that away. Earl! Is that you? Whatcha doing here? When'd you get out?" I said.

He grinned as his eyes skirted my naked body, like a starving man. For being on the other side of thirty I still looked pretty good. Bit of a pot belly but my C cups were still holding up.

"Whooo wee, a nude Tammi! Whatcho doin here, girl? Moved to the rich side of the lake? And ya, I got probation."

Prison had done Earl some good. I don't remember him being such a hunk two years ago. Thick bicep muscles flexed under his Soundgarden t-shirt. He'd grown a thick mullet, and added mutton chops over his acne-scarred cheeks. My knees were feeling a little weak.

"Put away for robbery, and you're out and at it again? You can't roll these folks. They're my clients!"

Earl put down his BB gun, and sauntered over to pull my towel away. I could feel my breath speeding up in a funny way.

"Clients? What kinda work you doing naked in this big ole house?"

I pulled his wife beater tank over his head. Fair is fair.

"I walk dogs, speaking of, how'd you get in? Django didn't yowl bloody hell?"

Earl leaned down and gave me a kiss, his mutton chops tickling my lips. He drew back and stroked my blonde perm.

"Came in the front door, didn't even know about no doggie. Dog walkin' pay well?"

"I make forty, even fifty bucks most days," I said, tugging down his camo pants.

"Oh, a sugar mama. You my dream come true Temptin' Tammi."

We tumbled onto the king bed, and it was even more satisfying than stealing a shower. I knew I was gonna spend the rest of my life with Earl by the end of those amazing ten minutes. Getting dressed, I told him how it was gonna be.

"Earl, you gotta put back the jewelry and make it look like we weren't never here. You can't be damaging my business."

At first he looked a little disappointed, but then gave me a little salute and sexy smile. I helped him put back everything, and straightened up the place. I still had a couple more dogs to walk, so Earl and I made plans to get together in the evening.

THAT NIGHT I put on my best tube top, feather earrings and Daisy Duke shorts where the pockets stick out on my upper thighs. We drove his scooter down to Mud Lake and spent the night under the stars. It was magical. I had beard rash on my face that would last for days. We cuddled up on a picnic bench.

"Tammi, you're my woman now," he said, puffing on a cigarillo.

I got a warm gooey feeling inside. I finally hooked myself a soul mate.

"I don't think Ma's going to let me move you into the Winnebago. It's not even a double-wide."

"And I'm bunking in with one of my roofer buds, it's not good for a class woman like you. We need to get our own place."

THE NEXT MORNING, I did the walk of pride back to my mom's trailer and changed into a spandex dog walking outfit. My body wanted to climb into my queen pullout. But Earl didn't have a job yet, and I had to keep earning the dough. I rushed through my walks that morning, not even bothering to steal a shower anywhere. Luckily, I had a few dollars saved up in an egg carton under my bed. Almost a G-note.

Earl was meeting me at the trailer dealer on the highway.

"A few guys owe me, so I'll collect and then we'll do some shopping," he promised.

My ma had a fair chunk of land, like an acre or two, and there was a patch down by the lake that would fit another trailer perfect. And far enough away, that if it got rockin', my ma wouldn't hear the talkin'.

Around 3 p.m., I put on my fanciest mini-dress, red with rib cut-outs, swiped on some pit stick, and shook some baby powder in my hair to degrease it. I borrowed Mom's old pickup truck with the bumper hitch (she was gone for the day, probably Bingo) and drove to Dick's Hitches and Homes to take a look.

Earl was already there, devastating smile on his face. Man he cleaned up good. "Here comes Temptin' Tammi."

His scooter parked to the side and his fine dark mullet in a braid down his back. He had on grey sweatpants and a nice denim cut-off vest.

With his shades on, you wouldn't even know he was walleyed. My heart fluttered.

"Let's find ourselves a castle, Prince Charmin."

We walked down the strip of dead grass between the rows of trailers. There were pop-ups, tear drops, fifth wheels, but they all had one thing in common. All way too much moola. Like over $10,000 for a tiny one. Earl brought a wad of cash, and between the both of us we had $1,700. I started to cry a bit, which wasn't good news for my blue mascara.

"Hey, I think I see a used bunch over there," Earl said.

I squinted though the makeup burning my eyes, and saw a hand-painted sign "Pre-Loved." We went to take a look at the three trailers sitting in the back. One was on blocks. One looked like it had lost a fight with a semi. The third looked good with road-worthy tires. Dirty, a bit lopsided, but not bad. Earl walked over to the hulking trailer.

"We've found ourselves a gem here."

He was right. Golden Falcon written on the front in fancy lettering, shoebox size windows everywhere and only a few broken bits. We walked around the side. There were two doors, a single solid one at the back and huge sliding ones with a duct-taped screen at the front.

"Look at the bump outs! There's already a kitchen table in here," I said, pushing open the front screen.

Earl knocked me aside in his excitement to have a look. I rubbed my ear where his elbow had accidentally whacked me, following him into the trailer. He was eager. I like that. The smell of dust, mold, and long dead mouse hung in the air. Faded linoleum and stained carpet covered the floor. Fake wood paneling made the insides shadowy and dark.

"I wonder what sort of stories this lady has to tell? Almost hear the porn and smell the weed," I said.

The way Earl ran his hand over the melamine counter in the mini-kitchen, he was sold. The best part? There was a full-sized bathroom in the back with a fine-looking shower.

"Yup babe, we found our new home. The Golden Falcon is gonna fly again," he said.

With that, we hopped out and went to find the owner of the yard. He'd seen us drive in and limped his way over from the office trailer at the front. A big belly, eight or nine strands of hair greasily plastered to his head and jaundiced skin.

"Hi! I'm Dick and I see you checking out our finest used trailers. So you folks wanna take this beaut home? Good deal! Just for today."

He stuck out a hand with dirty fingernails and I let Earl do the negotiating.

"Dick what's your best price? We'll take this baby off your hands right now."

"The only thing I gots to warn you about is the bedroom back door is jammed. But the rest of her works perfect." Dick said.

One thousand dollars and a few enthusiastic handshakes later, we were the proud new owners of the Golden Falcon. That left us $700 whole dollars to fix her up!

We hooked her up to the back of the pickup and hauled back. Thank goodness there were no cops out because the load was definitely illegal. The trailer rocked and shuddered as we slowly navigated the side roads. Luck was on our side and we managed to unhitch our new home in the dirt by the river.

My ma stood in the driveway bellowing "Tammi, what in tarnation! You can't park that ugly thing on my lot! Don't think you're hooking up to my hydro!"

Earl slouched down and pretended he didn't hear. He was a smart man.

She stomped down to the lake edge. My ma let me do what I want most the time. I'm her mini-me with the same long blonde hair, permed just right. Earl quickly unhitched the Golden Falcon.

"Better keep it clean outside," she said, climbing into her truck.

Well, those first days were plain bliss. We dragged my sofa bed down the hill, and Earl and I got down to the serious work of setting up our new home. Listening to our favourite hard rock bands, we ripped out the stinky carpet and bought a lime green shag from the thrift store. Earl managed to find a generator second-hand somewhere, so the beer fridge was humming. Plus the shower worked perfect once we put an old pump into the lake. My ma gave us a TV and VCR as a house-warming gift. After I found some vintage XXX movies on tape at a yardsale, we were partying like it was 1970!

Things didn't start going wrong until a week after we moved the Golden Falcon in. That day started as usual, I got up hung from cheap box wine and staggered to the other side of the lake to walk my dogs. Thank goodness the owners are normally at work. Django the Labradoodle and his designer breed friends never judge me for red-rimmed eyes. I survived the morning and went back home, looking forward to tumbling into Earl's arms (he hadn't found work yet) and perhaps having a beer to shake the cobwebs.

I stopped outside the duct-taped door. Terrible music blaring. I'm not a classical music fan but I could hear piano, string instruments, and horns. The Golden Falcon was pulsing with it. We listened to Slayer, not Chop chop or Beathaven or whatever. Storming in, I got my second shock.

"Earl! What have you done to your hair?"

Instead of drooling in bed with one hairy leg out of the sheets, my lover was sitting at the kitchen table writing on a pad of paper. His mullet was gone. All that lovely hair. He raised one hand to it, and stroked the neat business-like cut.

"I decided it was time for a new look. I don't want to stay a degenerate thief forever, my darling."

Darling? New look? Earl called me Temptin' Tammi. Not darling.

"What is this? We wake up to Metallica or Nirvana."

He kept writing on the pad of paper in front of him. I noticed he shaved. The mutton chops were gone, he wasn't half the sexy guy anymore.

"I find it inspirational; I had an idea for a story. Something re-envisioning the world with minimal light pollution and sustainable agricultural practices."

Sustainable what? Who was this guy?

"I'm going to go visit my mom, okay? Let you do your writing thing in peace."

He hardly acknowledged me, bending back over his notepad, grooving to his old-folk music. I grabbed two beers out of our fridge and walked the 200 metres to my mom's trailer. Stopping to look back at the Golden Falcon, I squinted my eyes. Did she look shinier? There was no way Earl had time to cut his own hair, shave and scrub the exterior of the trailer.

Instead of sitting down for a breakfast beer, I hopped into my mom's pickup truck and drove back to Dick's Hitches. The proprietor was out inspecting his mobile homes. Walking over to him, I noticed with disdain he was wearing a stained wife-beater tank top with a pair of dual-purpose swim trunks.

"Mr. Dick, may I have some discourse with you on the history and past ownership of our fine Golden Falcon?"

"Come again?" He squinted at me.

Come again was right. What verbiage was coming out of my mouth? I always hated people who spoke with high falutin' language. Thinking they were better than everyone else.

First my beloved Earl and now me! I concentrated and tried again,

"Who used to own that there trailer we bought from y'all a couple weeks ago?"

"Oh, some rich kids from a farm the next county brought 'er in. It'd been rotting in the field. They had a great-grandfather used to write poetry in it."

"And what happened to this author?" I asked.

Dick looked at me a moment, trying to access some dark compartment of his memory.

"If I remember rightly, they said the old geezer died in the trailer. He took to spending more and more time in there with his music and his typewriter and didn't come out for days. Was the smell that made them finally check on him."

Alright, thank you Mr. Dick, your time and consideration is much appreciated," I said giving his gnarly hand a shake.

Now, I generally don't indulge in superstition or believe in ghosts, but I had to do some thinking. I liked Earl the way he was before we started living in that trailer. No business haircuts and dumb ideas about writing stories about pollution or whatever. We were real down-to-earth folks, not the pretentious sort that lived on the other side of Mud Lake. I drove back to the Golden Falcon and noticed the screen was fixed. No duct tape. I could hear some Mozart playing from the boom box. (How did I know that name? Mozart?) My man was standing in the kitchen with a big garbage bag. I saw him tossing out my Cheesos, Mac n' cheese, frozen pizzas and cola.

"What are you doing?" I asked in horror.

He didn't even turn and look at me. His preppie hair cut made him almost unrecognizable.

"This is all garbage food, we are going to start eating organic and healthy. Farmer's markets, fresh produce. No more of this."

My jaw dropped open. This had to stop. The writing and haircut were bad enough, but an entire lifestyle change?

"I'm going out, Earl. My Cheesos better be back in that cupboard when I get home."

This time I drove into town to the hardware store. Turning up the radio loud, I tried to drown out crazy thoughts of going back to school and continuing my education. Perhaps as a vet tech? Or even a fully licensed vet? What a terrible idea! I hadn't even finished high school, there was no way I'd even get in.

Making sure I kept deranged thoughts at bay, I finished procuring what I needed from the hardware store. Then I drank a few beers and indulged in some fries at the pub until closing time.

Driving back to the Golden Falcon, I turned the truck lights out, the radio off, and drove up quietly. I needed to get my man back. The hot one with the mullet. I quietly opened the screen door and splashed gas over the green shag carpet. Then I lit it with a barbecue starter.

The whoosh sound and the flames roared up immediately. I stood back, the heat singeing my face. Like a bonfire, I could envision Earl and I warming ourselves, maybe roasting some marshmallows... Oh my God, Earl. What was I doing? I wanted to get rid of this cursed trailer, not him! It was the Falcon's fault everything was changing between us. I ran down to the bedroom door at the other end of the trailer and pounded.

"Come on out Earl! Fire!"

Nothing. I couldn't hear him inside. The fire was growing rapidly. The curtains and shag carpet went up like diesel fuel.

"Earl, you gotta get out!"

I wrenched on the door, but it didn't open. In a panic, I pulled and yanked harder.

"Fire, get outta there!"

The metal of the door was burning my fingers, I had to let go. The door hadn't moved an inch. I could hear Earl now and he was screaming.

Even though my skin was turning red from the heat, a cold wave of memory washed over me. Didn't Dick say something about the door needing to be fixed? The second one was jammed? My God, I just found the man of my dreams, I couldn't lose him now. I rushed over to the sliding glass doors, but its handles were glowing red. No touching them. The trailer was really flaming now.

Sitting on a lawn chair beside me, I noticed one of my super long dog leashes. Grabbing it I ran to the truck and hooked one end to the hitch. Then hopped in the truck and backed it up as close as I dared to the trailer. Looping the handle over the doorknob until it was tight, I hopped into the truck and gunned it.

The truck jerked when it ran out of dog leash and I felt the tires dig in. It only took a second or two before the whole bedroom door flew off the trailer body. Slamming on the brakes, I threw it in Park and got out. Earl staggered out of the trailer, coughing up a lung from all the smoke he'd inhaled and red welts coming up on parts of his arms.

I almost knocked him over running into him with a huge hug.

"Oh my Gad, Earl, you were almost barbecued. I love you so much."

He leaned over me and gave me a huge squeeze back, the smell of ash and fuel stinging my nose.

"My Temptin' Tammi, you saved my life woman."

We stood back a few metres from the blazing trailer, now not much more than a burned-out shell, and watched the flames slowly die down. We didn't have much in the Golden Falcon to burn. A few of the other residents of the park wandered over. Some with beers, others in their pjs. My ma came up to stand beside me.

"Is there even a point of calling the fire department now? Looks like that she's gonna be nothing more than cinders and a shell before they'd even get it," she said pointing her cigarette at Earl and I. "You two are gonna have to pay to get what's left of that eyesore towed out of here.'"

Earl hugged me tighter, he was okay, done coughing, and the red arm spots just needing some aloe.

"Yes Ma'am. Tammi and me, we'll clean up this mess. We ain't got no insurance so I guess we back to where we done begin," he said. "I must have fallen asleep smokin' or something."

His words were like music to my ears. I wasn't sure if he knew the fire was my fault and he was taking the blame—or if he genuinely didn't know. No matter, I was his Temptin' Tammi again and my Earl would grow his mullet back if I asked nice. I reached up and gave his scarred smoky cheek a kiss.

"Guess you're both spending the night with me then. Y'all have to look for a rental in the morning. I think my cousin might have a base-ment apartment in town he'd put you in for a good price," my ma said, turning and walking back up to her place.

I grabbed Earl's hand and smiled at him. We both needed to clean up, and I guess we were going to have to make do with my mom's tiny bathroom. But Earl and I had our whole future ahead of us. Who knew? Maybe this basement apartment would have a nice big shower with room for two.

9

———

ABOUT "THE LAST RIDE"

~

First published: October 2019
The Corona Book of Ghost Stories

Inspired by the Twilight Zone, this is a ghost story with a non-neurotypical main character. Sometimes what makes us different can be our strength. Who doesn't find Ferris wheels creepy?

10

THE LAST RIDE

BY ANGELIQUE FAWNS

Sabrina stared up at the abandoned Ferris wheel. It loomed forgotten on a run-down section of Myrtle Beach. It was impossible to tell what colours may have once decorated the swings sitting on the rusty frame. Dust and decay coating any memory of the laughing passengers of years ago. The crowds had migrated to the modern SkyWheel located on the popular Oceanfront Boardwalk and Promenade. It had a completely different feel to it. A metallic monstrosity which carried passengers in gondolas and soared an unbelievable height into the clouds.

Sabrina didn't like riding the SkyWheel. Being in a small enclosed space made her feel claustrophobic. Just one of the many phobias she dealt with on a daily basis. In fact, there was nothing she liked about the popular tourist area. The crowds made her feel panicky. At seventeen years old, she could be the poster child for mental health issues. Even now in March, after the school break crowds had gone back to class, it was still sensory overload. Cars blared music and cruised the main drag until all hours of the morning, some even with the modified shocks that made them jump up and down. Mothers hollered at over-sugared kids tearing up and down the beach.

A cool wind was blowing off the ocean tonight, making the open-air chairs rock and creak. This area was one of her favorite places to walk in the evening. There was something soothing about the boarded-up vacation cottages and decrepit boardwalks deemed not worth fixing after the last hurricane. They were damaged. She was damaged. Her ponytail had loosened and the strands were blowing into her eyes and face. Pulling the band off, she tried to tuck her hair back into its tight configuration. It took her three tries. Everything took her three tries. Every light switch had to be flipped three times. Her shoelaces tied three times. When she was typing her school work, she read over every paragraph precisely three times.

Her peculiarities really didn't start to manifest until puberty hit. As a child, they just thought she was quiet and shy. Then as a tween she became plagued with panic attacks and obsessive compulsive behaviour. Her parents hauled her to doctors and psychologists. The diagnosis was mild Asperger's syndrome, something they had missed when she was younger. She zoned out in the office when the doctor was explaining everything, so Sabrina googled it later. Basically, you have normal intelligence and language, but impairment with social skills and prone to repetitive or restricted behaviour. Yup, that was her in a nutshell. She did go to therapy once a week to work on her communication and develop coping techniques, but honestly, it felt like a waste of time.

How could she explain why she had to do almost everything in a multiple of three? She tried to give her mother and friends a physics lesson. How three was nature's favourite number. That there are three types of stable neutrons: The proton, the neutron, and the electron. And how all solid matter is made of atoms built entirely from these three particles. Science explained her OCD perfectly – one good thing she got out of high school. Everyone else was missing the logic. So she checked the lock three times after shutting the door. Brushed her teeth for exactly six minutes. Thirty-three strokes of her hair every night.

Of course, she got teased at school because of it, or just ignored. There were a few kids who tolerated her, and she even had one close friend who found her quirky and fun. Deirdre started hanging out with her in seventh grade, and never minded waiting while Sabrina zipped and unzipped her coat three times. Now they were both in grade eleven, and Deirdre's social life had blossomed while Sabrina became even more introverted. She had been invited out tonight with Deirdre and a few others to go to Applebee's for snacks. Sabrina felt ill thinking about the Friday night crowds at the chain restaurants. Plus, she hated watching the other girls roll their eyes when Sabrina started removing the ice cubes from her Sprite until there were exactly three cubes (or six or nine) in her glass.

Instead she was here, alone, staring up at a depressing amusement ride. She lied to her parents and told them that she was joining Deirdre for the girl's night out. Her folks were relieved whenever she put down a historical romance novel (her favourite escape) and went out like a normal teen. Her curfew was a reasonable – 11:00pm, so that gave her plenty of time to stride the deserted streets finding relief in the fresh air and solitude.

She was about to start her loop back home, when the Ferris wheel creaked and started to slowly rotate.

"What! Is anybody there? Is this a trick?"

Peering through the gloom, she couldn't see anyone at the base of the old amusement ride. In fact, there was a chain-link fence around the perimeter to discourage playing or climbing on it. The terrible creaking sound tore at her eardrums.

"Hello? Is anyone over there? This isn't a good joke!"

No one answered. Sabrina took a closer look at the chain-link and found that someone had pulled up a section just big enough for a small person to crawl through. Dropping to her knees, she slithered through the opening, swearing when a bit caught and tore her jacket. The Ferris wheel was picking up speed, and she could hear soft music.

Getting closer, she noticed the Ferris wheel wasn't as decrepit as she first thought. The music got louder, a fun jazzy piece. Then laughter and chatting. Sabrina closed her eyes and gave her head a shake to clear her ears.

When she opened her eyes, things REALLY didn't make sense. The sun was shining, people were milling everywhere and a five-piece band was rocking out under a big white gazebo. It was like a scene from one of her historical romance novels. The Ferris wheel was shiny with fresh paint and every seat was full. Ladies in frilly dresses, fascinators, and parasols sat delicately as they were whisked around and around. Kids laughed beside them, while men kept one arm around their dates and another on their hats.

Sabrina stood there with her mouth open. What was this? Had she slipped, hit her head, and was now lying in the dirt? Taking her hand, she pinched her arm, three times, hard. Yes, it hurt and yes, she was still standing in a world that had transformed itself into a lively and lovely day at an old-time fair. How many times had she read her novels and wished she could be whisked into the pages?

"Ma'am step right up! We have a seat for you right here," a young man in a colourful suit called to her.

The Ferris wheel slowed down and an empty chair stopped at the bottom. Sabrina hurried up the steps to the platform and took the young man's proffered hand. If she was dreaming, she might as well enjoy a ride. He helped her settle into an empty car, and shut the safety bar tightly.

"Enjoy the view, ma'am, and have a lovely day! We hope you stay a while," he said with a big grin and a quick bow.

The Ferris wheel started back up again, and it was glorious. The sun was warm, and the view was spectacular. There were no garish signs advertising tourist attractions, no big freeways, just trees and perfect little houses with the ocean glistening nearby. A small boy in the car in front of her turned backwards and waved at her enthusiastically. Sabrina felt happy.

After several rotations, the Ferris wheel slowed, stopped, and Sabrina's car rocked gently at the top of the structure. Must be time to load on new passengers.

A woman in the chair behind her shouted, "You can stay here forever if you want!"

Sabrina turned and saw a lovely young lady in a yellow frilly dress and matching feather hat.

"You can live here with us and ride the Ferris wheel whenever you want!" the yellow lady said.

"How can I do that?" Sabrina asked, feeling excited. She didn't want the ride to end.

"You just have to jump," said a man in a dapper blue suit from the front car. He must be the child's father.

"What? How does that make any sense?" Sabrina asked.

"You can stay here forever. We have fun everyday!" his son said, bouncing on his knees in the seat.

"Yes, stay with us Sabrina, join us Sabrina, we want you Sabrina..." all the riders on the Ferris wheel started to chant.

The sound of their voices and the rocking of the Ferris wheel in the breeze seemed almost hypnotic. What would she be going home to? A life where she was lonely? Where she never fitted in?

"Just jump, Sabrina, and you can have fun forever in this wonderful world," the yellow-dress lady said.

Yes, she could stay here forever. Like living in one of her books. She started pushing up the safety latch.

The voices got more excited as the sounds of the band faded. "Yes Sabrina, join us Sabrina, jump Sabrina..."

She raised the safety bar up once and brought it back down again. Then she did it for a second time.

"Hurry Sabrina, we are so hungry Sabrina..."

Her hand paused as she heard the voices chanting. Hungry? She looked away from the latch toward the lady in the yellow dress. Except this time her dress was ripped and black. And her face was no longer peach perfect with rosy cheeks. Bones peeked out from decayed flesh. The little boy was grey with teeth missing and one eye lolling out of its socket. Clouds had passed in front of the sun and shadows darkened the fair.

Sabrina gasped and shoved away from the safety bar. She had been just starting her third unlocking of the latch. The final unlatching.

"Damn. Too greedy." The ghoul turned back into a pretty lady and smiled at her. The music swelled again and the clouds passed on. "Come on Sabrina, you will love living with us!"

Sabrina pushed her body back against the seat and took a tight grip of the bars. She couldn't believe how close she had come to jumping. Would she have been committing suicide? Keeping her eyes screwed tight, she counted to twelve. When she opened her eyes, it was night again, and she was sitting in a rusted old car swinging at the top of the Ferris wheel. The people, the music, and the old town were gone.

She could hear was the whistling of the wind, and the distant roar of the interstate, but no brassy band. How had the Ferris wheel moved? If she wasn't a hundred feet in the air, she could have told herself she imagined the whole thing. She didn't have her cell phone on her. She'd wanted solitude so had come out without it, as for sure Deirdre would be calling her, telling her to come join the crowd. So, she couldn't phone anyone for help. There was no one on the streets to call to, and she definitely didn't want to spend another minute on this haunted contraption. Looking down, she saw that there was a complicated configuration of bars and struts holding the ride together. It looked climbable. Taking a deep breath, she crawled out of the car and slowly made her way down.

Where those hands plucking at her t-shirt? The metal was cold and rough under her palms, but she hung on tightly and scrambled down. A few little cuts started bleeding on her palms where stiff peeling paint and rough metal nicked them.

She thought she could hear a whispering in her ear, "Jump Sabrina, let go Sabrina, it would be so easy..."

Distracting herself, she envisioned the atoms of the Ferris wheel in groups of three and muttered to herself, "We have three atoms, which become six, which become nine, which become twelve..."

She still imagined cold hands and voices, but she could become completely distracted when she counted atoms. Grunting and concentrating, she made her way down to the ground. As soon as her feet hit the dirt, she scrambled back under the fence and turned around to look back. The antique cars swung slowly and hypnotically in the breeze, but they weren't rotating. Shuddering, she swore to herself that was the very last time she would ever ride a Ferris wheel. As she started walking away there was a whisper in the breeze.

"Come back Sabrina... we will be waiting..."

11

ABOUT "THE GARDEN PARTY"

~

First published: September 2019
Cursed Collectibles

Shannon Fox is a guest author in this collection, and her creepy tale of curiosities in an antique shop is brilliant.

Shannon is a multi-genre writer of stories spanning past, present, and future. Her work has appeared in several publications, including *DreamForge Anvil*, *Air & Nothingness Press*, and *Third Flatiron*. When not writing, she spends her time dancing with horses which she's found is significantly easier to do with four feet instead of two. She lives in San Diego, CA, with her husband and three cats – one of whom may or may not be a demon in disguise.

Visit her at www.shannon-fox.com.

12

THE GARDEN PARTY

BY SHANNON FOX

a stone angel clutched a laminated placard between its fingers: 50% OFF! EVERYTHING ON SALE! Moisture had smeared the corner of the red ink.

"Let's go in," Charlie said. He pulled Katie by the hand towards the entrance of the store.

She dug in her heels when she saw what kind of store it was and rolled her eyes at her boyfriend. "Really, babe? Another antique store?"

"Just for a minute. Just to look."

"No," Katie said. "I told you I wanted to go home. My feet hurt from walking, I'm sunburned, and I've got sand all over me."

"You're the one who wanted to go to the beach," Charlie said. He looked her up and down with a smirk. "To get a tan."

Her blood pounded in her ears as she felt the judgment leeching into his words. *Pale people don't tan, so why did you even bother trying?* She wanted to smack the smug look from his perfectly bronzed face.

Charlie let go of her hand and took a step towards the store. "Stay here if you want, but I'm going in."

She watched the door shut behind him and contemplated

storming off towards the car. She wondered if he'd chase after her. Or if he'd even noticed she'd moved from the sidewalk outside.

Katie looked at the sign in the window as she pushed open the door. A.R. Gread. She was sure Charlie was in hog heaven to be browsing a store with a snooty name like that.

Dusty armoires and curio cabinets cluttered the floor, their shelves crowded with curiosities. Paintings of all styles and sizes clung to the walls like fungus. What couldn't be hung up was simply leaned against wrought iron tables and rolled up oriental rugs. Statues jockeyed for the last remaining bits of floor space.

Katie wrinkled her nose at the musty odor. She hated that smell. It was the scent of too many afternoons wasted while Charlie haggled over a lamp or an old book.

As she made her way deeper into the store, she was careful not to touch anything. She knew firsthand how serious these shopkeepers were about their "You break it, you buy it" policy. With her student loans, she didn't have any extra pocket money to spend on this place.

A group of small, white porcelain figurines lined up on a table caught her eye. Her grandmother had owned something similar. She'd actually left the collection Katie, but Katie had given it to her little sister. At the time, she hadn't had any use for miniature kittens and puppies with dopey smiles on their faces. Now, though, she wondered if perhaps she should have kept one to remember her grandmother by.

As Katie reached for the tiny white horse in the corner, a disembodied voice startled her.

"Is there something I can help you find?"

Katie looked to her right and spotted a man seated in a red velvet armchair. She hadn't noticed him as she'd walked up. Probably because he looked like one of the antiques himself.

Though the thick bush of white hair adorning his head revealed his age, his blue eyes were sharp and his face was curiously free of wrinkles. His skin had the unnaturally smooth look of a shirt that had just been ironed.

"I'm just looking," Katie said, hoping he would go away. She didn't like the way he was looking at her. As if she were a chocolate he wanted to pluck from the box. She needed to find Charlie and get out of here.

As if he'd been summoned, her boyfriend rounded the corner with a canvas in his hands.

"This painting is incredible. Who painted this?" Charlie turned the canvas around, so the shopkeeper could see it. In her opinion, it looked like a passable attempt at recreating a puddle of spilled spaghetti sauce.

The shopkeeper stood. "That was done by one of our local artists. I can find the name if you'd like."

"Please," said Charlie.

When they were alone, Katie grabbed Charlie's sleeve. "Can we go? I'm tired."

He shook her off without glancing at her. The painting had his complete attention. "Just a couple more minutes."

"I think I got too much sun today," Katie said. "I should lie down. Please, let's go home."

Charlie sighed. He set the painting down and turned to her with narrowed eyes. "You always want to leave."

"Not always," she protested.

"I never complain when you make me go to the mall with you to purchase yet another lipstick that you're just going to lose in the bottom of your purse."

"When was the last time we even went to the mall? We've been to four antique stores this weekend alone!"

"I haven't found what I'm looking for yet."

Katie folded her arms over her chest. "And what's that?"

He threw up his hands. "You wouldn't understand."

"I wouldn't? Do you even know what you want? Where does it end, Charlie? With us spending every weekend arguing in antique stores, over and over again until one of us gives up or dies?"

Charlie pointed a finger at her. "You always turn it into a fight."

"You never listen to what I want."

"Because you don't compromise. If you'd just let me have five minutes to look around—"

"We've been here longer than that. At least ten minutes."

"Because you're distracting me, Katie. How am I supposed to take a good look around with you constantly whining and pulling at my sleeve?"

Katie gritted her teeth. "I do not whine."

"Excuse me." The shopkeeper smiled politely at them. "The name of that artist is Timothy Pollard."

Charlie nodded, as if he knew exactly who that was. Katie rolled her eyes.

The shopkeeper took a step towards her. "You didn't seem very impressed with the painting so I thought you might like this instead."

She heard Charlie gasp as the old man turned the object he was holding in his hands to face her. It was an antique silver mirror. The filigreed handle was tarnished in places and the surface of the glass was spotted with age. But worse than the imperfections of the piece was the face staring back at her in the mirror.

To her horror, Katie now saw that a bloom of pink colored her cheeks and nose. Her freckles, which she tried to keep concealed under layers of carefully applied makeup, had multiplied exponentially in the sun. Strands of blond hair hung limply around her face like greasy noodles.

Katie tore her gaze away from the mirror. She had to get home before someone she knew saw her like this. "Charlie, we're leaving." She tried her best to sound assertive, as if her words brooked no argument.

But Charlie either didn't hear her or didn't care. In his hands, he now held a ceramic elephant. About the size of a grapefruit, it was stylized and covered in a mosaic of colorful tiles.

She knew why it had caught his eye; Charlie used to have a similar one. Until Katie had knocked it over on their first anniversary and its destruction had seriously brought into question whether they would see another year.

"How much is this?" Charlie asked, turning to the shopkeeper.

"I'm afraid that one's not for sale."

"How much, though? One hundred dollars? Two hundred?"

"I'm sorry, but it isn't for sale."

"Two-fifty?"

"Let's go, Charlie," Katie said. She raised her voice. "I mean it. It's me or that stupid elephant."

But her boyfriend continued to ignore her and took a step towards the shopkeeper. "Come on. Everything's for sale for the right price. Just give me a number. I'm not leaving without it."

A cloud of dark smoke suddenly stung Katie's eyes and made them water. She squeezed them shut and coughed as the smoke tickled her throat.

When she opened them again, the smoke had cleared and she was alone with the shopkeeper. Charlie was nowhere to be seen. On the carpet, the ceramic elephant lay on its side.

"Charlie?" She looked around but didn't see him anywhere. She hadn't closed her eyes for long. How could he have moved that fast?

The shopkeeper stooped to pick up the elephant from the carpet. It seemed to shimmer as he laid his hands on it. A trick of the light, perhaps.

"Did you see where my boyfriend went?"

The old man shrugged. "You said you wanted to leave. Now you're free to go."

Katie blinked. "You didn't answer my question."

"Didn't I, though?"

"Where's Charlie?" She hated how her voice quivered as she said his name.

In response, the man turned and walked away from her, heading deeper into the store.

"Hey!" Katie yelled as she followed him. "I was talking to you."

The shopkeeper glanced over his shoulder at her but did not stop until he was standing in front of an enormous curio cabinet. He unlatched the doors and Katie could see that there was empty space on the top shelf, just wide enough to accommodate a ceramic elephant.

"What do you want with this man, anyway?" the shopkeeper asked as he slid the elephant onto the shelf where it belonged. "There are other, better specimen."

The elephant glittered in the late afternoon sun.

"Other, better specimen?" Katie asked. "What happened to Charlie?'

There was a twinkle in the shopkeeper's eye as he smiled. "I think you know what happened to Charlie."

She looked from the cabinet to the man and back again, a pit of dread growing in her stomach.

"What have you done?"

"You gave him a choice. He chose."

"He's not…"

"Dead? No. Not dead. Suspended. Like a mosquito in amber."

"But he's inside that elephant?"

"His soul is."

Her pulse pounded in her ears and she felt dizzy. She wanted to believe the man was lying to her, that his mind was simply addled by age. But what other explanation was there? One moment Charlie was there, demanding the man give him a price for the elephant and then, with a puff of smoke, he was gone.

"He didn't deserve this," she said. "Not at all."

The man looked annoyed. "You're deceiving yourself, Katie. You were there. You told him to choose you or the elephant. I'm sure that wasn't the first time you've felt as if your own existence paled in comparison to the latest trinket or artifact he happened to stumble upon. No, I'm sure this has happened many times before."

He was right. Katie knew he was right. But she loved Charlie with everything that she was.

"Give him back." She felt her hands curl into fists at her sides but forced herself to relax. Attacking the old man wasn't going to make him any more inclined to help her. And she needed his help to get Charlie back.

"I'm afraid I can't. I never intended for it to be reversible." His tone was so certain, so final that she knew he wasn't lying.

Katie stared at the Charlie-elephant in the curio cabinet as tears blurred her vision. What was she going to do now? She couldn't just leave him here. All alone, sandwiched between a gilded tiger and a monkey in a fez hat. Her eyes kept moving along the shelf, taking in the crocodile with its yawning jaws, the parrot with ruby eyes, and on and on. She gasped.

"They're not...all of them?"

The man gave a curt nod. "But don't mistake them for people who deserve your sympathy. Every one of them stumbled in here, blinded by their greed, and quite willingly walked into the trap I laid."

She thought she might be sick as her eyes roamed around the antique store, taking in the sheer number of figurines packed onto shelves. There must have been hundreds of them.

"It's not just the statues," the man said. "Everything you see in this store is enchanted."

Katie put a hand out to steady herself as the blood roared in her ears. Hundreds upon hundreds of people just like Charlie. "Everything? How could you do this to them?"

"Imagine a garden party, Katie. One with plates of finger sandwiches, fresh fruit, colorful macaroons, and pitcher after pitcher of iced tea. A lovely event that can only be ruined by one thing," the man said. "The inevitable arrival of a cloud of buzzing flies, drawn by the aroma of food. You can't stop it from happening. Unless, perhaps, you catch them first. I find a jar of honey to be quite suitable for such an occasion."

"Is that how you describe it? Catching flies with honey? Those are *people* in there."

She took a breath. For courage. "And I suppose I'm next."

He shook his head. "No, Katie. You're free to go."

She stared at him, searching his face to see if he was joking. "Free to go? Why not me?" she asked.

"Why not you? Because you're a guest at the garden party, Katie."

She squeezed her eyes shut. They'd been planning their wedding. Charlie had told her he was shopping for the perfect ring. She'd begged him to buy her something modern, not anything that came from a glass case in an antique store. They'd fought over it, but in the end she'd won that round. After all, if she was going to have to stare at the ring every day for the rest of her life, it needed to be something she liked.

They had vacationed with each other's families. They shared a bank account. They'd been looking at condos together. They were planning to get a puppy in the fall. Everything was going according to plan.

And yet. Now she was free to go, free to walk back into a different life. A life without Charlie, yes, but loving Charlie had never been easy. She had always come second to whatever item he'd toted home from the flea market. The brass candlesticks, the first editions, the porcelain figurines, all of it capable of eliciting more affection from him than she ever had. She remembered the stinging slap he'd dealt her after she'd broken his elephant. She could almost feel the way his hand had closed around her wrist, squeezing until she thought he would snap it. The wild look he'd had in his eyes as he'd yelled at her and called her all kinds of vile things. When he kissed her, those words still returned again and again to her mind, no matter how hard she tried to forget them.

A few tears slipped down her cheeks, stinging her sunburned skin. As she wiped them away, she suddenly thought of Morocco. A place she'd wanted to visit for years. But Charlie had always said no, had always said traveling outside the country cost too much.

Katie blinked her tears away and promised herself she would go. She would see the markets of Marrakesh. Visit a sultan's palace. Ride a camel through the desert. Do all of the things she'd always wanted to do now that she had no one to tell her no.

"Do not misunderstand me," the man continued. "You're certainly flawed. You're vain and at times, selfish. But you're not disposed to greed. Not as he was."

"Is greedy really the worst thing a person can be? And who are you to judge?"

She watched the shopkeeper's face as he considered her words.

He suddenly looked very, very tired and she wondered how old he was. And what he was.

"I have walked this Earth for a long time. Longer than you can fathom. Greed brings war.

"It tears people apart. It causes love to wither on the vine. Perhaps greed is not the worst of all sins, but it is among the most destructive.

"As for who I am, it is irrelevant. It does not change his fate."

She took a breath. "I don't understand why you'd let me go, after everything I've seen here today."

He shook his head. "Once you walk out that door, you will never return. This place won't open for you. It was intended for Charlie."

"But I walked in on my own."

"You were accidentally caught up in the enchantment. Like one of those fishing nets you humans are so fond of using. Now I'm releasing you. So go home, Katie."

She hesitated, just for a moment. Then she pointed to the Charlie-elephant. "Not without him."

"I can't let you do that."

Katie crossed her arms over her chest. "You can and you will."

Amusement glittered in his eyes. "Are you threatening me?"

Her insides turned to ice at his words, but she fought to keep her voice steady as she replied. "Not a threat. You said it yourself: what's done cannot be undone. So it won't matter if he stays here with you or goes with me."

The man rubbed his chin. "It has never been done before. I don't know that his soul will continue to live on if you take him from this place."

"Then I would be doing him an even greater kindness."

The man studied her for a long moment, appraising her like one of his antiques. Katie forced herself to meet his gaze, though her skin crawled from his attention.

After a long moment, he nodded. "You are the first person who has ever been unintentionally caught in my trap. So I suppose it's only fitting that you will be the first person to ever remove an object from my store. If you understand the risk to Charlie and wish to proceed anyway, I will let you take him with you."

She nodded. "I have to believe he truly loved me. And that he would do the same if our roles were reversed."

The shopkeeper unlocked the curio cabinet and picked up the elephant. He stroked its trunk for a moment, before placing it in her outstretched hands and gently folding her fingers around it.

"It is not my place to speculate on human relationships," the man said. "But I agree he loved you. As he loved all the objects he possessed."

With that, Katie suddenly felt a crushing pressure in her skull as the man and the shop around him twisted, blurred, and disappeared.

She found herself standing on the sidewalk out front, facing an empty storefront, with the elephant in her hands. It was still late afternoon and the sunlight reflecting off the mosaic of tiles that formed the elephant's hide momentarily blinded her. She blinked against the glare and slipped the elephant in her pocket.

The statue of the stone angel still stood out front. Its hands, now empty of the laminated placard, beckoned to her.

The shopkeeper had said that everything inside the store was enchanted. She'd taken that to mean that the figure outside was just a normal statue. But as she stared at the orphaned statue of the angel, she felt a shiver run down her spine and walked quickly away. Perhaps it wasn't enchanted as the others were, but there was still something unnatural about it.

On the way back to the car, a window display caught her eye. The TV screen inside displayed the words "Nobody loves you like you do" in bright, rainbow colors. She'd never noticed this store before. Perhaps it was new. Katie watched the TV until the words faded out and were replaced with the brand's logo: Vanity Outfitters.

Katie felt as if she'd been plunged in ice water. She glanced down the street toward where the antique store had been.

Could it be?

She closed her fingers around the elephant in her pocket and turned away from the window.

13

ABOUT "INKED FOR LOVE"

❧

First published: October 2021
Accursed

THIS STORY FEATURES a protagonist in love with a bad-boy biker. But you know what they say... be careful what you wish for. Another comedy horror offering with a hint of romance.

14

INKED FOR LOVE

BY ANGELIQUE FAWNS

*H*er entire body was covered in art. Even with her employee discount at Taboo Tattoo, it had cost her a fortune. Hearts seeped rivulets of blood down her soft white arms, roses with sharp thorns decorated sturdy legs, black swans hugged her chest, and snakes slithered down her back. Lily was into bad boys, and thought she'd found her soulmate. He just didn't know it yet. Snake was only interested in her as his tattoo artist. She was losing sleep and going crazy dreaming of the big, heavily-tatted man with hypnotic eyes. There was nothing she wouldn't do to get him, including finding herself in a dodgy part of the city in the wee hours of the morning.

The shop was called Pagan Possibilities. It could only be accessed off an alley strewn with used needles in the Queen Street West area of Toronto. The shop had once been a garage, and still showed signs of it. Paint peeled from the aluminum siding, and a window was blacked out. The smell of cannabis hung in the air like long dead skunk. Lily clutched the shop's worn flyer in one sweaty hand, trying to summon up the courage to enter. She hoped this was the right place. The literature said the shop was only open from midnight till 3 a.m. on Friday nights, so she had hopped on a streetcar and braved drunks, hookers and opioid users to try her luck.

Fingering the stud in her lip, Lily took a deep breath, pushed open the door and walked in. Licorice incense tickled her nostrils. A low glow came from crystal lamps and candles and the décor could only be called hoarder-chic. Jars filled with murky liquid, candles, incense holders, garden gnomes, pentacles, hundreds of books, and bedazzled shawls fought for space on every dusty shelf and table. Lily picked up a jar, but quickly put it down again after seeing toad heads floating in the liquid.

"Hmm, there is something you desire. Something you want more than anything in the universe. You think I can help you," said a gravelly voice from the dark.

Lily saw a hunched figure in a dim corner of the garage behind a desk and started squeezing past overflowing tables. As her eyes adjusted to the gloom, she saw the proprietor of Pagan Possibilities wasn't hunch-backed, but wearing a set of wings and a positively stunning black lace gown.

"Hello darling! Look at you! Those are some amazing tattoos, and I positively love the purple hair. I'm Penny and this is my little shop of horrors and wonders," she said, one hand on a slender hip, the other twirling a piece of her long black wig.

Lily looked in astonishment at the store owner. She was gorgeous. A serpent-like body, muscular and sensuous, with soft dark eyes, and only the faint shadow of a beard on her face.

"I was at a summer solstice party with some of my Wiccan friends and found this pamphlet. I'm desperately in love with a man who comes to my tattoo shop and my heart is gonna explode into a million bloody pieces if I can't have him," Lily said, pointing to a tattoo of a shattered heart on her forearm. "Like this."

"Well, you've come to the right place, I have some powerful potions, but if you're a tattoo artist, I have a really extraordinary ink. But let me warn you girl, once you needle this into someone's skin, they will be yours forever. Be sure or beware," Penny said as she reached beneath the desk and brought out a small container of scarlet liquid.

Lily looked in fascination at the iridescent red ink. It slowly swirled and curled in the clear plastic tube.

"It almost looks alive! I'll take it. How much?"

"Three hundred dollars, but make sure this is what you want," Penny cautioned.

Lily was already seducing Snake in her mind, and quickly counted out 300 dollars in large bills. She handed it to Penny as she tucked the ink into her pocket. Hustling out of there, she went back to her apartment above the tattoo shop to catch a few hours of sleep before her favorite client arrived at noon the next day.

WHEN SNAKE WALKED into the shop, sweat started to trickle down Lily's armpits. She was wearing her most flattering skull and crossbones mini dress, and had made a special effort to flat iron the long purple hair on the unshaven side of her head. Six feet tall, with a gym-toned body, long black hair caught back in a man bun, and startling green eyes, he was the most gorgeous human being on Earth. Luckily, he was addicted to ink, and came in at least once a month to get a new tat, or add some color to an older one.

"Hi Lily! I'm looking to add something special to my arm sleeve today. Maybe a dragon? A bloody sword?" Snake said.

He untucked his black t-shirt from his tight Levi's and pulled it off. Lily greedily drank in the wide back, taut muscles, and artistic ink covering most of his upper body. She had done most of the work, and a world of castles, dragons, swords and starships already decorated him.

"How about something special today? I designed this just for you," Lily showed him a drawing of a large skull whose teeth clenched a rose dripping blood from the petals.

"That's fantastic. Put it on my tab, and let's do it," he said as he settled into her chair.

Lily knew he was good for the cash so she took out her special tube of scarlet liquid and poured it into the ink cap. It came out in thick globs and looked like it was breathing as it pulsed in the gun. She found a clear place on his forearm and started working on his skin with the tattoo needles. Breathing in his smell of Irish Spring soap and sweat, butterflies started their familiar flapping in her belly. How many nights had she lain awake imagining her thighs wrapped around his motorcycle as she pressed her lips into his back? Then looking into his eyes over a bonfire as they sipped whiskey?

The hum of the machine masked her excited breathing as the black skull with the red rose appeared beneath her fingers. A tattoo of this size took her around four hours, but the minutes flew by. The longer she could be near Snake the better. She paid special attention to the flower, making sure the ink was extra vibrant. This tattoo was going to be the most important work of her life. After Lily carefully cleaned the reddened skin, she tried to put a bandage on it, but Snake flapped his hand at her.

"You know me baby, I live dangerously. Let it breath, "

Snake pulled his t-shirt back on and studied her for a minute, "you know, you look different today. Really beautiful. There is something... I don't know. Do you want to go for dinner with me tonight?"

"Yes," Lily gasped, that special ink worked fast. The skull on his arm seemed to wink at her and the blood streaming off the rose looked wet and alive.

"It's four now, what time do you want me to come get you? I almost don't feel like leaving you, I kinda want to just stay here and stare at you"

"Now! I can go now, you're my last client of the day, the benefits of being self-employed," Lily said, "let me grab my purse and we can get some pre-dinner cocktails."

She followed him out of the shop then locked the door behind her, unable to believe her luck. The newly created skull watched her from his arm. She shook her head, it must be an illusion. No tattoo was actually alive. Snake walked down the sidewalk and stopped at a touring bicycle locked to a metal post, with a helmet hanging off the handle bars.

Lily's jaw dropped, "I thought you said you rode a mean bike."

"Yes, this is a top-of-the-line Schwinn. Want me to double you? Or do you have your own wheels?" Snake said, flashing her his devastating grin. "You are gorgeous, those curves and that purple hair. I don't know how I didn't notice before!"

Lily stared at the five-speed, not sure what to say. This put a kink in her Sons of Anarchy fantasy.

"Here, climb up on the seat and I'll stand and peddle. I'll take you to my place. I got some beer in the fridge and we can figure out where to go for dinner," he said, looping one long leg over and leaning into the handle bars to make room for her.

She climbed up behind him and tried to enjoy holding onto his broad back as he push-pedaled them down the road. At least the guy was environmentally conscious. Though it was only about a ten-minute ride, her dress got wrinkled and her butt was sore when they showed up outside a small semi-detached brownstone. They both tumbled off the bike.

"Wait till you meet my Mom! You're going to love her. Hey, maybe she can make us dinner tonight and save some money?" Snake said walking quickly up the driveway after dumping his bike onto the lawn.

"You live with your mom still?" Lily asked as she hustled after him. "Aren't you like thirty-years-old?"

"Thirty-five actually. She's divorced and likes the company. Besides I'm between jobs right now, so it works for me," Snake pushed open the front door.

"How long have you been unemployed?"

"A couple years, but I'm working on an app. Hey Mom, come meet Lily! She's my tattoo artist!"

Lily followed him, noticing the photos of a young Snake (he definitely had a dorky, pimply stage), and crocheted art informing guests that "Hookers Do It With One Hand" and "I Crochet Past My Bedtime."

A grey-haired lady came out of the kitchen smiling, "Snake, I'm glad you've finally brought a girlfriend home! I was beginning to think you played for the other team."

"Mom, don't embarrass me. I'm taking Lily down to the basement okay? Maybe you can bring us down some snacks?" Snake said, turning to descend a narrow set of stairs.

"Nice meeting you," Lily said to the still grinning lady as she awkwardly followed Snake.

Getting to the bottom of the twisty stairs, she took in the Star Wars posters, big video game console, ratty couch with a 70's flower pattern and weight set in the corner. The smell of dirty gym socks and mildew was overpowering. Lily felt her heart sink. This wasn't quite how she envisioned her first romantic encounter with the man of her dreams.

Snake was leaning into a beer fridge and pulled out two bottles of Michelob Ultra. "Here you go Lily. Want to play some Mario Cart?" he asked, tossing one to her.

Lily twisted off the top and took a long guzzle. Maybe she could save this.

"Not big into video games, but I hear there's gonna be a rave on the beach tomorrow night. They're bringing in a DJ and everything," she said.

"Tomorrow? I can't. That's my Dungeons and Dragons night. You can come play with us if you like," Snake invited.

Lily stared at him. He played fantasy board games? Maybe she couldn't salvage this. He drank his beer in long swallows and the newly inked skull was laughing at her now. She had been picturing dinner in an exotic restaurant on King Street, with candles flickering as they supped oysters—knowing what that would lead to later. Not mom-made snacks in a man-boy's basement. Where were all his sexy friends who gave themselves tough nicknames?

"How did you get the name Snake?" she asked.

"Oh, my name is Stanley, but when I was younger, I was really good at Snakes & Ladders," he said plopping himself down on the filthy torn couch.

"So, Stanley, I'm gonna to have to get going. Sorry to cut this date short."

"Hey, when can I see you again? I go to my Cosplay Club on Sunday, I bet you'd fit right in," he said jumping to his feet, "do you need me to double you back on my bike?"

Lily was already walking up the stairs, but stopped, "Cosplay? What's that?"

"You dress up as really cool characters and act like them, sometimes make mini-plays. I never miss Comic-Con."

Lily blinked. She wouldn't be caught dead dressed up as a comic book character. She continued up the stairs and called over her shoulder, "No need for another bike ride, I'll catch a cab."

She could hear Stanley's mom in the kitchen, but slipped out the door without saying goodbye. Lily was disappointed, how did she read him so wrong? Tears streamed down her face as she walked down the driveway. Snake lived in his parent's basement, was unemployed, and played Dungeons and Dragons? And here she thought she was going to be a biker's "old lady." Lily wiped away her tears and started laughing. She stopped walking and had to hold on to a lamppost to keep herself up. She laughed and howled and then sunk to her bum leaning against the pole, completely drained.

After ordering an Uber she went home and fell into an exhausted sleep. For the first night in a long time, she did not dream of rolling around with a naked Snake.

THE NEXT DAY, Sunday, she had a group of five bridesmaids, along with the bride, come in to get matching ankle tattoos of pink butterflies. She was on the third lady when a ruckus broke out on the sidewalk outside the shop.

"Hey! You've gotta see this! It's Star Wars out here!" one of the waiting women shrieked.

Lily put down the tattoo machine and rushed to the window. There were seven people dressed head-to-toe in white Storm Trooper outfits doing a dance routine with a portable stereo. A crowd was gathering on the sidewalk.

The performers were carrying big black toy guns and making a huge racket shooting them and doing high kicks.

The tallest one stopped and yelled, "Lily this is for you! Your Snake LOVES you."

Lily wanted to disappear in embarrassment. The bridesmaids covered their mouths and giggled. Out on the streets a couple of news vans showed up. The local news channels were filming the gathering crowd and the Storm Trooper's antics. Taboo Tattoo was supposed to be edgy, dark and mysterious. A group of dancing cosplay Storm Troopers were not helping with that image. Her boss was going to be furious, and now it was on the news.

She tried to ghost Snake as he sent her text after text that week, ignoring every message. But he didn't give up, instead he showed up outside the shop in various costumes begging her to come over to his place for a Mario Cart marathon. One day he was a Power Ranger, the next The Green Lantern, the third time Deadpool. The week went by excruciating slow as she waited for Friday to arrive.

Finally, she took the streetcar to Pagan Possibilities in the wee hours of the morning and rushed into the garage as soon as the door was unlocked. If anything, there was more paraphernalia littering the occult store. Lavender incense was burning.

Penny sat behind the desk, a private little grin on her face. She had seen the dancing Storm Troopers on the news and heard the declarations of love and devotion. Once again, the magic ink had done its job.

"Penny, you have to reverse the power of the ink! Snake is not who I thought he was, this guy lives in his mom's basement and doesn't even have a job," Lily blurted.

"I told you to be sure before you imprinted him with it. You were warned," Penny said, ruffling the green ballroom gown she was wearing.

"I can't live with this. I don't want to spend my weekends playing fantasy games and travelling by bicycle. Plus, he's scaring off my customers! He shows up wearing cosplay costumes and it's really uncool."

"The special ink is much like regular tattoo ink; it will fade in time and so will its power. You'll just have to be patient. Snake will slowly lose his obsession with you."

"What do I do in the meantime?" Lily asked leaning over the desk, eyes wide in desperation.

"Join his Cosplay Club? Learn to love Dungeons and Dragons?" Penny chuckled.

15

ABOUT "TREATS"

First published: October 2019
Rigor Morbid: Lest Ye Become

ROBERT STAHL IS a guest author in this collection, and his Halloween-themed tale has a frightening twist.

UNBEKNOWNST TO ROBERT STAHL his body is an empty shell, telepathically controlled by a brain in a jar which was buried long ago under the floorboard of his home in Dallas, Texas. Consequently, his days are filled with the urge to write: stories, letters, articles, whatever. At night he listens to music, and when he finally drifts off to sleep, the brain laughs, a humorless, pitiful sound as it jiggles alone in the dusty darkness. www.robertestahl.com

16

___

TREATS

BY ROBERT STAHL

Bernice Jones stared down at the pumpkin she had just carved. Frankly, the damn thing gave her chills. There was something sinister about the triangle eyes glaring back at her, something dangerous lurking behind that jagged, crescent-moon grin.

Normally she went for more cartoonish faces at Halloween, but moments ago something had come over her. She had seized the knife powerfully, arthritis be damned, and her hands had taken on a life of their own, slicing quickly, almost manically, through the pumpkin's dense flesh. Well, scary or no, the jack-o-lantern would have to do. Trick-or-treaters would be arriving soon, and she hadn't time to carve another. She wiped the sticky pumpkin guts off her fingers, dropped a candle down into the hollowed-out belly, and carried the jack-o-lantern out to the porch. *Halloween*, she thought, *was there a gayer holiday in the whole world?*

Bare autumn branches made skeletal silhouettes against the sun's harvest glow. The leaves had fallen early this year due to the brutal summer—the driest since the heat wave of 1954. That year had been a doozy. She'd lost her husband, Harold, that same year. Hard to believe he'd been dead ten years already. A sudden gust of wind slammed the door shut, jerking her out of her thoughts. A handful of leaves whirled around in an invisible vortex. Odd. Up until then, the day had been still. But that was the weather for you. No matter what the muck-mucks on TV said, you never knew what it was going to do.

Bernice eased the jack-o-lantern down onto the stoop and took a few minutes to survey her decorations. Tonight of all nights, everything had to be perfect. She readjusted the scarecrow in the rocking chair. Just this morning, she'd made it by stuffing some of Harold's old clothes with hay. It made her feel like part of him was with her again. She stroked the collar on the torn flannel shirt lovingly before stepping into the yard. There, she untangled the sheet ghosts flapping under the elm tree and fluffed the cotton spider webs blanketing the bushes. Real spiders gave her quite a fright, but the artificial webs added just the right touch of spooky drama.

Back in the kitchen, she filled a bowl with the best sweets she could find: Tootsie Rolls, Zagnuts, and Turkish toffees. Nothing cheap, like candy corn and butterscotch. Halloween wasn't the time to skimp on treats. The neighborhood expected a certain level of quality from Bernice, from the prize-winning pumpkins she grew in her garden, to the candy she handed out to the trick-or-treaters. Even parents from other neighborhoods carted in their children by the truckloads to ring her doorbell. Now, Thanksgiving was a fine holiday, full of warmth and spirit, and everybody loved Christmastime. But for full on magic and excitement, Halloween took the cake.

"It was a one-eyed, one-horned, flyin' purple people-eater," she sang as she smeared on green face paint and slipped into her costume. Then, after plopping a pointy hat on her head and lacing up her boots, she retired to the couch with a glass of sherry.

ON THE PORCH, the wind started up again.

It spun in tight circles, lapping up leaves and dust motes, taking on substance and density, forming into a dark cloud.

The cloud zigzagged close to the jack-o-lantern, hovered over it...

...and seeped into the open mouth.

Flames licked out of the face.

On Bernice Jones's porch, something woke up. Something powerful and evil and as old as the world.

The pumpkin moved. It started as a wobble. Then slowly, smoothly, the jack-o-lantern rotated to face the door, its eyes glowering with a palpable sense of malice.

The cloud billowed out of the pumpkin and oozed out into the lawn, working downward, seeping through layers of topsoil, leaving behind the still bodies of ants and grubs, their tiny hearts instantly frozen.

It continued on, into the roots of the elm tree.

The root cells felt a spurring to wakefulness as the cloud passed through. Though they hardly moved all year 'round—except for a few centimeters of growth now and again—they were moving now. They twitched and wiggled, pulled themselves taut, and strained furiously against the taproot. One by one, they tore loose. They squirmed through the earth, blind as worms, and popped up through the grass. Near the porch's edge, they gathered, and twisted around one another like snakes.

A fibrous shape started to form.

First, a torso. Then arms. Legs.

On the lawn, a gangly figure now stood. One of its feet tore loose from the earth, came down again. The other followed suit. The figure took several shaky steps and then stopped.

It was missing something.

Sinewy arms plucked the jack-o-lantern off the porch, set it down squarely on the shape's shoulders. The sigh of old magic lifted into the chilly air.

A neighbor came shuffling down the sidewalk. Doris Haversham gawked at Bernice's decorations, paying particular attention to the terrifying new creature with the pumpkin head on the porch. *Bernice has outdone herself again*, Doris thought, before making a few mental notes for next year's decorations and hurrying home to tell her husband.

The creature watched, silent as a gravestone. Then it shuffled over to the scarecrow and worked its wiry fingers curiously over the moth-eaten fabric.

~

THE DOORBELL RANG at 6:15 p.m. Bernice yanked the door open and cackled her best witch's cackle, but stopped suddenly. Her next-door neighbors, Brian and Judy Hanson, smiled back at her, dressed as a coal miner and a nurse, respectively. Their daughter, Lauren, stood close by, dressed sweetly as a princess in a ruffles and a tiara. She took a look at Bernice's face and shrieked before lunging behind her father. Bernice whisked off the hat. With some extra candy and a cookie from the cupboard, she coaxed the girl into smiling again.

It wasn't until the Hansons were waving goodbyes from the sidewalk that Bernice noticed the missing pumpkin. A pile of strewn hay marked where the scarecrow once sat. The clothes were gone, too. *Teenagers*, she thought. They were the worst part about Halloween. Already with the pranks, and it wasn't even night yet.

She was sweeping up the last bits of hay at dusk when an early group of trick-or-treaters came ambling down the sidewalk. There was just enough time to hurry back inside, put the hat back on, get into character.

When she opened the door again, she gave it to them good, waving her hands as if throwing a spell and cackling for all she was worth. One of the kids dropped his bag, he was running so hard.

It felt good to be back in the game.

Night came, bringing lots of trick-or-treaters. They came dressed as pirates and vampires, werewolves and skeletons; they came as cheerleaders, devils, and fairies. Pick-ups and station wagons cruised the streets, letting children out, picking them up again. Parents called out to the youngsters in the darkness, urging them not to run, to watch out, to say thank you, to not drop candy wrappers on the lawn.

But as Bernice's feet became sore inside the boots and the last pieces of candy rattled in the bowl, she'd knew she'd had enough. It would be nothing but older kids from now on. They always came later, rarely in costume and usually without a proper treat bag. She didn't have the patience for them, not after what they'd done earlier. She flicked off the porch light and lowered the shades.

The makeup came off easy.

AT A QUARTER PAST NINE, the doorbell rang again. Bernice sat on the couch, her belly warm from all the sherry. She crept to the door and gazed out through the frosted glass. A lone figure stood on the darkened porch.

"No more candy," she called through the door.

The figure shifted, listening. The doorbell rang again.

She swallowed hard. "Go away."

After what felt like a long time, the figure slunk off into the darkness.

She double-checked all the locks in the house.

When she picked up the sherry glass again, her hands were shaking.

Ring-ring.

The doorbell again.

On television, Cronkite was rambling on about the Soviets, which meant it was almost 10:30. Bernice glanced at the blinds to make sure they were closed. She held her breath and tried to make her body small. Best to simply ignore the knock until they went away. Except, the sudden burst of light on the porch wouldn't let her.

It looked like...flames?

She hurried to the door, yanked it open.

Her doormat was on fire!

Rather, not her doormat, but a grocery bag sitting *on top* of her doormat. Flames chewed through the bag's paper walls. Blackened bits of ash broke free, did somersaults on the evening breeze.

This prank, she knew. Stamp out the fire and end up with a shoe covered in dog shit. They'd done the same thing to Doris Haversham down the road last summer. The little jerks were probably out there now, watching her. Well, she wouldn't give them the satisfaction. She snatched up the doormat and slapped it against the bag until the fire went out.

She smelled it in the smoke. The shit.

The laughter of teenage boys drifted out of the shadows. She heard sneakers hitting the blacktop as they ran away.

Good riddance to the no-goodniks.

When she returned with a bucket of water, she didn't feel angry anymore. She remembered being that age—too old to be trick-or-treating, too young for that mischievous streak to have worked its way out of your bones completely. She'd smashed her share of pumpkins back in the day, egged plenty of garages.

She was remembering those days still as she tucked herself into bed, and the sherry put her to sleep before long.

A DARK VEIL fell over the neighborhood.

At the rear of Bernice's house, a spindly figure lurked in the shadows, barely visible except for two burning triangles of light that reflected in the glass of the kitchen door. Gnarled hands twisted the doorknob.

The door was locked.

But underneath the knob, a keyhole.

The fibrous tangle of roots that made up the hand separated. Several of the thinnest filaments lengthened and slipped into the hole. The lock clicked and the door creaked open. The figure lurched inside, its crude feet scuffling faintly on the kitchen floor.

It stopped in front of the sink. A knife gleamed in the moonlight, drying on a towel, a thin thread of pulp still clinging to the blade. The hand curled around the handle, picked it up.

Perhaps the knife would carve again soon.

~

BERNICE TOSSED and turned in her sleep.

In her dreams, a shadowy monster pursued her. She ran, but the only place she could find to hide was a graveyard. She was ducking behind a tombstone when a thunderclap woke her. It took a moment for her eyes to adjust.

Candlelight flickered in her room. Strange. She hadn't lit a candle before going to bed.

The light was coming from her doorway, where a solitary figure stood.

Someone in a costume?

Was it a costume? The body seemed too thin to be human. Stranger, its limbs appeared to be made out of tangled vegetation. Vines, maybe? Natty clothes engulfed the intruder's gangly frame. Even weirder, he was wearing...a jack-o-lantern mask?

No, not a mask. She could see no head inside. Only a burning candle, the light of which filled the room with a baleful glow.

Those empty, burning eyes watched her.

This wasn't any jack-o-lantern. It was *her* jack-o-lantern.

The intruder's breathing rasped throughout the room—quick jagged bursts, like the panting of a tired dog. Something smelled foul, like rotting leaves. The intruder held a knife. *Her* knife. It was streaked with what appeared to be red paint.

What kind of creature was this?

She tried to scream, but the cry hung in her throat. She struggled to move, but her muscles resisted. Had the creature paralyzed her?

The phantom creature shambled forward, its movements stiff, as if in mockery of the human form.

Near the dresser, the thing paused. Something had caught its attention: A porcelain ghost figurine, one of Bernice's favorites. A hideous laughter filled the room, and the creature smashed the figurine against the wall. "Halloween," an ancient voice croaked. "Do you even know what that means?"

The voice echoed off the walls but also seemed to be coming from inside of her.

"Bernice Jones, do you know why pranks happen on Halloween?"

The creature knew her name, could read her thoughts. But what kind of a question was this? Halloween wasn't anything to think about. It was simply one of autumn's rituals, something you just did.

The phantom's voice continued: "On this night, the membrane between our worlds is thinnest, allowing *my* kind to visit to *your* world. It's nothing for one of us to slip inside the skin of a mortal and spread a little chaos. Those boys who started your fire earlier, what do you think got into them?"

It couldn't be true. Halloween was just a silly tradition, wasn't it?

"There's so much you don't know about Halloween, Bernice. But I'm going to teach you. Yes, Halloween is so much more than candy and costumes."

Hellish light filled the room as the eyes flashed brighter. Bernice saw movement near the footboard. A black finger, curled over. No, not a finger. A bristly, hairy leg. Seven more came into view, exactly like the first.

A tarantula! She hated spiders more than anything.

The tarantula's swollen body crept onto the sheets. It was massive, the size of her hand, horrible and black against the white of her comforter.

Another tarantula jumped on the bed, near her feet.

A flash of lightning illuminated the dark corners of the bedroom, revealing tarantulas everywhere—hundreds, maybe—writhing and quivering on the walls, leaping on the lampshades, streaking across the dresser.

Something scurried over her leg. Eight cruel eyes flashed in the darkness as the first spider scrabbled the length of her body, venom dripping from its fangs.

She closed her eyes to pray.

A bristly leg touched the bare skin of her throat.

With the force of her scream, the magic that held her let go. She bolted upright, flung the spider wildly away.

When the lighting flashed again, the spiders were gone.

But not the creature.

It was lumbering toward her.

She tore from the bed, pulling over the nightstand in hopes of slowing the creature down, and bolted for the hallway.

The creature's footsteps were right behind her as she hurried into the kitchen. The knife hissed through the air, the blade slicing through her nightgown, nicking her shoulder.

She reached the doorknob, but her hands shook too much to get the lock open. If she could get outside, call over to the Hansons, shout to anybody who could help her. Even the boys from earlier, if they were still out there—!

A fibrous hand came down over her mouth. She whirled around to face her intruder.

What the creature wanted was for her to follow it.

Though terror made her legs quiver, she trailed the lurching figure through the back door and into the yard. Wind howled through the treetops, whipping her nightgown around her frail body. In the rot-black sky, the waning moon struggled to shine through a mass of storm clouds like a cataract-covered eye.

The creature led her to the path at the rear of her property, past the dilapidated shed where she kept her tools, and into the garden. In the summers, she planted her pumpkins here, but the vines now were yellow and sagging. Any other time, she felt happy here. Tonight the place filled her with dread.

The creature jerked up an arm and pointed a warped finger toward the patch.

She felt herself stepping forward, soggy earth sucking at her cotton slippers.

The clouds shrank away, and the garden filled with silvery moonlight. She'd been wrong: some of the plants lived. Some even bore pumpkins. Strange, since she'd harvested them all days ago.

"Glory, no," she gasped.

Doris Haversham's vacant eyes stared out from a tangle of leaves, and her tongue lolled out over a sagging jaw. The skin at the neckline was torn, jagged. The heads of Brian and Judy Hanson had been stuffed under a nearby plant as well, next to their daughter's head. A tiara sparkled on her forehead.

There were heads under all the plants, dozens of them. Neighbors, most. People she'd known for years.

The wind picked up, bringing a sound that filled her heart with dread. At the garden's edge lay an expanse of woods, lush and green in the milder months but now soulless and haunting with the onset of autumn. Hundreds of wailing voices were coming from that direction, crying out in pain and misery. From the shadows, a host of dark entities emerged. She saw shades and specters and hairy beasts with blood-matted fur. There were armor-plated bugs with snapping claws, pulsing things with beaks, and oozing blobs with snaking tentacles. They descended from the sky as well —witches on broomsticks, shrieking banshees, and slobbering beasts with leathery wings.

Every horrible, make-believe monster she'd ever imagined was here, and they were coming for her.

Unable to bear the spectacle any longer, she fell to the earth and hid her face with her hands, but the sound of her crying was drowned out by the wailing horde and the hideous laughter of the pumpkin-thing.

THE NEXT MORNING, she woke in her bed, drenched in sweat. Pulling back the comforter, she found her nightgown spotted with mud. As she traced the dirty footprints to her back door, the memory of last night returned. She raced for the garden, bracing herself for what she would find.

Everything was as it should be. No heads peeked out from the pumpkin leaves. Not a solitary pumpkin grew on a vine.

She found her jack-o-lantern on the kitchen table, the candle inside burned to a nub. The knife lay on the counter, just where she'd left it. A fog settled in her brain, a confusion unlike anything she'd ever experienced. What was real, and what wasn't? Why was it so hard to tell the difference?

Soon after, Doris Haversham passed by on the sidewalk, whistling while she walked. Her head was still intact. Later, Brian Hanson honked on his way home from work. He seemed cheerful, had even waved.

She'd dreamed it, that was all. A nightmare. But one so vivid, she'd gotten out of bed, gone sleepwalking. Yes, that had to be it.

So she thought, until she found the knife-shaped rip in her night-clothes.

Something unholy *had* visited her. A terrible, malevolent force from another world had entered her home and delivered its message. A laugh started up deep inside her chest, starting as a mirthful giggle before growing into a maniacal shriek.

Halloween.

She'd been doing it wrong all this time.

A YEAR PASSED.

On Halloween day, she got up early, just like always. She ate a good breakfast and spent a few hours making sure the decorations were in order. Then she opened her pantry, hauled out the bushel of apples. She'd been buying them all week to make sure she'd have plenty. It was Halloween, after all. Tonight, everything had to be perfect.

She strolled out to her shed, piled a stack of boxes under her chin and took them inside. The objects in the boxes, you had to handle carefully, but oh, how those sharp edges glittered when they caught the light.

A big night lay ahead. Time to get to work.

"It was a one-eyed, one-tailed, flyin' purple people-eater," she sang, working the first of the razor blades meticulously into the yielding fruit flesh.

Yessirree, tonight would be one for the books.

17

ABOUT "A COLD SLITHER KILLING"

First published: March 2023
Heavy Metal Nightmares

REVENGE IS *a dish best served musically. Especially if that music is inspired by Alice Cooper.*

18

A COLD SLITHER KILLING

BY ANGELIQUE FAWNS

It was a coincidence that Michelle has just confessed to Glenna when the incident happened.

"Call me a fan of shock rock, but I absolutely love Cold Slither. The lead singer Gary Groody? He's my guilty pleasure," Michelle had said, a half-smile pulling at her glossed lips.

"Me too." Glenna gave the tanned girl's water tube a little shove. "Now I know you have the best of taste in men and music."

The 13-foot boa constrictor, Crush, was known for escaping from bathtubs when travelling with Gary Groody's entourage. The snake slid off the concrete boulder on the edge of Lake Ontario at the public beach. Glenna and Michelle were giggling at their newfound shared passion when the disturbance of the water rocked the pink tubes. Michelle screamed when the wedged head surfaced several inches from her hand. In her panicked struggle to get away from the snake, she somersaulted into the water.

Glenna laughed and rolled onto her stomach, watching her bikinied companion sputter and splash. Michelle's pure white bathing suit became see-through in the water and was obviously more for show than function.

"Would you look at that! How on earth did a Boa Constrictor end up here? You're pretty far from home buddy." Glenna trailed her hand after the ringed tail.

"Forget the snake, I can't swim." Michelle desperately tried to keep her nose above water. Her black painted nails clawed at Glenna's tube, her own having drifted several feet away.

Glenna balanced on her knees on the edge, adjusting the straps of her one-piece Speedo. "You're shitting me, right?"

Michelle couldn't answer. Her head dipped beneath the surface, black hair pooling on the oily surface of the lake. Glenna looked at the beach. There were a few people enjoying the warm fall day, but no one was looking their way. Sighing, she dove into the water but didn't immediately grab for her friend. Michelle's eyes were open under the water, the whites of her eyes unnaturally wide. Bubbles streamed out of her mouth.

Her arms slowed their thrashing.

Michelle sunk a few inches lower into the darkness.

Glenna swam behind Michelle, wrapped her arms around her torso, and hauled her to the surface. Michelle was still, limp in her arms.

Glenna kicked away from her water tube, swimming for the shore. Huffing, she strained her leg muscles. Michelle's dead weight was harder to haul through the water than she had imagined.

Michelle gave a shudder, violently coughing and spraying water out of her mouth and nose. She walloped Glenna in the head.

Glenna held her tighter. "Stay still, or you'll drown us both."

Her black nails gripped her forearms so tight there would be bruises tomorrow. Michelle still wiggled, but stopped the violent fighting. Glenna was able to swim faster. Struggling up the pebbly shoreline, she removed Michelle's death grip, and rolled her onto the sand. Her chest shuddering, Michelle rested on her hands and knees, coughing and gagging.

The few people on the public beach still paid no attention to them.

Michelle glared at her with red-rimmed eyes. "How? Why? Were you going to let me drown?"

Glenna shrugged. "I thought you were joking. Who can't swim these days?"

"Me." Michelle got slowly to her feet, marched over to where they had left their bags, and left the beach without saying another word.

"See you at work tomorrow." Glenna called after her.

Michelle ignored her.

THE NEXT DAY at the radio station, Michelle pointedly looked in the other direction when Glenna passed her reception desk. Glenna pursed her lips as she walked past the elegant main office into the bowels of the station. She knew she had to do something to repair the friendship. Really, the only reason she had given up her job as a morning drive anchor at CRNB 108.3 in Muskoka was to make friends with the pretty receptionist.

The public relations team had received some comped tickets to the Cold Slither Concert tonight. It took some flirting and several pointed hints, but the station manager finally came through. He gave her two tickets.

As he walked away from her desk, Glenna smothered her scream of excitement with one fist and drummed her feet on the floor. A couple of her fellow schedulers gave her dirty looks from their cubicles. There were areas of the radio station filled with music and laughter, but not in the administrative wing. Everyone here was hunched over a computer frantically assigning numbers to commercials and slotting them into appropriate on-air breaks. Filling in the daily log for Rock 999 was a deadly boring job. She often seriously questioned leaving her dream job working on-air in Ontario's cottage country. But she had an agenda. A deadly serious one. These two Cold Slither tickets, casually tossed onto her desk with a wink, were just what she needed.

These tickets were in the corporate area. Bigger seats, free drinks, and one of the best views in the house. Under the canopy. Attending concerts at Ontario Place could be dodgy. A few seats were under shelter, but many were on the grass. Toronto's notoriously rainy fall season could make sitting on a blanket, miles from the stage, miserable.

How was she supposed to concentrate now? Her heart was pounding in her temples. Her calves were throbbing. She rushed the last few inserts for tomorrow and logged out of the S4M program she was using. Making sure none of her co-workers were paying attention, she pulled up her Facebook page and scrolled through her own feed until she found a picture of her sister. They had their arms flung around each other and were drunkenly raising glasses of beer at a family reunion.

What a coincidence that "The Bloody Hunt" was playing in her headphones. She kept her eyes on the time stamp on the TV forever tuned to the 24-hour Toronto news station. As soon as it flicked to 5:00pm she felt her pulse quicken. Yanking the buds out of her ears, she ran down the twisty staircase while clutching her concert tickets in one hand. The building was state-of-the-art. Frames decorating the wall holding records for bands that had gone Gold and Platinum. Cold Slither had six platinum albums on the wall. She stopped at the receptionist's desk and waited impatiently for the Michelle to get off the phone. How did she spend all day answering calls and never smudge that black lipstick? Michelle dressed goth chic, and looked equally good in the black jeans and tank top she was wearing today as she did in that white bikini yesterday.

Glenna subconsciously smoothed her hands over her conservative skirt. Another downfall to working the corporate side. The dress code. In Muskoka, when she was the morning show talent, she could wear whatever she liked. Most of the time she wore cargos and a plaid shirt. Perfect for Northern Ontario. They all liked to joke, she had a great face for radio.

Michelle was still ignoring her, answering the phones, and doing her shtick. Her friendly grin and sexy voice charmed clients and co-workers alike. The executives loved her pretty presence at the front desk.

"Hey, I have some comped tickets for Cold Slither at the Budweiser Stage tonight. Wanna join?" Glenna asked her.

Michelle gave her a dirty look but looked interested. "Cold Slither tickets, eh?"

"Look I am so sorry about the Lake Ontario thing. I honestly didn't know you couldn't swim. Let me take you out. Make it up to you."

Sweeping her purple hair out of her eye, Michelle let a smile touch her lips. "I do love Cold Slither."

"All is forgiven?"

"You did save my life. It just took you a minute." She was fully grinning now.

"Cold Fucking Slither, right?"

Michelle jittered with excitement. "You mean Gary fucking Groody!"

"It's on baby, all is forgiven?" Glenna put her hand up for a high five.

"For Gary? All is forgiven." Michelle gave Glenna's hand a whack back. "Netflix will have to wait! I'll meet you just outside the ticket booth on the hill at Ontario Place? It's four now, I'm off in an hour."

Michelle made rock hands and stuck her tongue out.

"My logs are done, so I am going to sneak out now. Time to dust off my hair crimper!" Glenna cheeks glowed triumphantly.

GLENNA FOUND Michelle exactly where she said she would be, sitting on the hill by the lake at Ontario Place. She flopped down beside her; happy she wore jeans as she watched Michelle yanking on the short leather skirt riding up her thighs.

"Wow, you went retro." Glenna appraised the studded bracelets, Doc Martin boots, and thick chain necklace.

Michelle laughed. "Channeling my inner-goth. I haven't worn dog collar jewelry since high school."

"It suits you." Glenna pretended to strangle herself. "Wow, where did you dig up that head shop jewelry?"

"Back of the closet baby, I love your outfit too."

"Classic, right?" Glenna ran her hands over her Cold Slither T-shirt. "Shall we really do this old school and pre-drink?"

She pulled two paper bags with tallboy beers in them out of her purse.

"Absolutely." Michelle took a bag.

"Let's get away from the gate. Don't need a public drinking ticket." Glenna winked.

They ran, giggling, towards a bridge over Lake Ontario on the far side of the amphitheater. The complex sat on the edge of Lake Ontario. Green rolling hills, white building popping up like daisies in an award-winning architectural masterpiece.

Michelle hummed a few bars of "The Snake is Hungry" then swallowed a sip from her can.

Glenna admired Michelle's cool way of pouring her beer from the bag into her mouth without touching the mouth of the can. She tried to do the same, but it dribbled down her chin.

Wiping her face, Glenna leaned over the railing. "This place reminds me of my sister. We used to come here and watch Disney movies at the Cinesphere." She nodded to the big orb beside the music stage.

"You have a sister? You've never talked about her." Michelle leaned precariously over the bridge, staring down at the dark water.

"Well, she died, so I don't talk about her much."

"I am so sorry. When?"

"Last year, right before I moved back to Toronto. I had a radio show in Muskoka, but I left it to work for Rock 999. She was going to the University of Toronto for her Masters." Glenna finished her beer and gave Michelle another one.

Michelle gratefully accepted it and took a long swallow. She avoided Glenna's eyes. "Death is such a bummer."

"That's one way to put it." Glenna watched her companion fidget.

Michelle became quiet, the energy seeping out of her like an invisible succubus had latched onto her. She was looking at the dark water, lapping softly around the piers of the bridge. There was the faint smell of seaweed and long dead fish on the breeze.

Michelle leaned right over the bridge rail. "Do you ever think about throwing yourself off?"

She was hypnotized, swaying a bit. Her long purple hair hung over her cheeks and her lean torso teetered precariously on the railing.

"Like you lose your sanity for a moment and a compelling force makes you want to hurtle yourself over?" Glenna dug her nails into her palms.

From the open-air stadium the first chords of music rang over the water. Probably the opening band. Glenna wasn't a huge fan of Cold Slither's opening act, so she didn't mind if she missed them.

Michelle didn't answer Glenna but kept talking in a dreamy voice. "Sometimes when I'm driving on a cliff or bridge, I want to do it. Drive off the edge. I want to crash. I want to jump."

"Like an uncontrollable impulse?"

"No. Like a punishment." Michelle looked away from the water, met Glenna's eyes and bit her lip.

Glenna put her arms behind her back and forced a smile. "I get it! I'm afraid I will end up possessed and just for one moment some evil entity will take control of my body and hurdle it over for me!"

Michelle's eyes had tears in them, but she wiped them away. "Umm you're weird. Demonic possession, eh? That's not what I am talking about. I think I deserve it. I want to throw myself off but I don't, not brave enough."

Glenna let that hang in the air, keeping her eyes cast down on the cold lake.

"Alright, I'll bite. Why do you think you deserve to die?"

"What would you do if some bitch was making moves on your man?" Michelle tugged on a strand of purple hair.

"What would I do? Or what would Gary Groody do? Use a guillotine obviously." Glenna tried to joke.

Michelle grabbed her hand. "What would you do?"

Glenna wiggles her fingers away from Michelle. "Trust my boyfriend to choose me. And if he doesn't, then why would I want him?"

"Chuck is pretty freakin awesome. Basically, a Gary Groody look-alike. Long blonde mullet, can rock the vinyl pants. Sometimes you got to fight for your man."

"So, what about this bitch?"

"Her name was Kim. My best friend. Drinking, smoking, hanging out. But then Chuck told me she tried to kiss him."

"Was? Her name was Kim? Why past-tense?" Glenna voice dropped an octave.

"She slipped and fell one day; we were going for a hike along the Scarborough Bluffs." Michelle threw her empty beer can into the water.

Glenna shook her head at the littering. "So, Kim slipped, did she? Was she clumsy?"

"Nope. Like a mountain goat." Michelle leaned out further over the rail and wiggled her fingers at her King beer can floating towards the boat docks. Her heavy bracelets made a clanking sound.

Glenna looked at the back of Michelle's head, that sleek purple hair, and clenched her teeth. Michelle was teetering again, balancing her slightly inebriated self on the railing.

Glenna took a deep breath and clenched her fists, this time drawing her own blood in her palms. Should she do it? Could she do it? This was why she had given everything up. Left a dream job in Muskoka for a logging job in Toronto. This was the moment. Her "Vengeance is Sweet" (only Cold Slither's best song) moment. Plus, she said she deserved to be punished. Glenna agreed. She unclenched her hands, took a step towards Michelle, and gave her a push.

Michelle's light body flipped easily over the railing.

"Ahhh!" She shrieked, plummeting with a splash into the icy lake.

Glenna looked around quickly and was relieved to see nobody around. Unlike at the beach, the shore was truly deserted. Everyone was at the concert by now. She examined the water for any sign of a black dress or purple hair. That heavy chain jewelry. Those big Doc Martin boots.

The seconds passed impossibly... slowly... and then Michelle's head broke through the water. Black mascara streamed down her face and she screamed at Glenna.

"You pushed me! The water is freezing." Michelle's head bobbed back beneath the water.

Glenna waved at her, a smile slowly spreading across her face.

"I can't swim." Michelle sputtered, water bubbling out of her mouth.

She was desperately trying to keep her nose above water. Her black painted nails clawed at air, those thick necklaces allowing only her lips to breech the surface.

"I know, you told me at the lake, remember? I saved your life." Glenna leaned over the rail; her belly pressed into the cool metal. Relishing the cold feel of the steel. Feeling a strange peace.

"So, save me again, you can swim." Michelle's head tilted way back, water filling her mouth at the edges.

"I don't think so, I don't rescue snakes." Glenna spat into the water, the glob landing beside Michelle's purpling face.

"Help--" She submerged completely.

Her purple hair pooled on the surface, then disappeared as Michelle sunk.

"Kim was my sister." Glenna said to the ripple of water. "Chuck was her boyfriend you common cuckoo. You stole him from her."

A few bubbles formed a circle on the oily water. Glenna stepped back from the railing.

The dark water remained still.

She tilted her head, listening... No sounds from the water, but she could hear the roar of the crowd. The opening act must be done. Her heart swelled as the volume soared. Heading back down the bridge, Glenna hummed along with her second favorite Cold Slither tune. She could hear the opening chords of "Sometimes the Rat Has to Die."

She picked up the pace, she wasn't missing this concert for anything. Those corporate tickets weren't going to go to waste. She would just tell people Michelle stood her up. She was always going on dates with random guys, everyone would believe this time Michelle met her Mr. Goodbar. Not every guy was a nice guy. Like Michelle had tried to tell Kim. Chuck was no good.

After the concert she might work overseas. She knew of a radio station in Australia on the beach in Mooloolaba. Or why go that far? There were lots of media companies in San Fransisco. Basically the birth place of thrash metal.

Her steps got lighter the closer she got to the Amphitheatre, dancing to the recognizable licks of a Cold Sliter tune. She especially loved his routine with the Boa Constrictor. Apparently, Gary had to get a new one for this concert. Crush had finally escaped for good. She punched a fist into the air, celebrating Crush. In Glenna's opinion, snakes belong in the water.

19

ABOUT "MEMO FROM THE JOLLY OVERLORDS"

First published: December 2020
Weird Christmas Podcast

R.J.K. LEE IS a guest author in this collection, and his short festive tale is terrifying and delightful at the same time.

R.J.K. LEE (HE/HIM) immigrated to Japan in 2005 from Oregon, USA. He's puttered along train tracks to meet quotas for the overlords ever since, currently as teacher, proofreader, and voice narrator, while churning out fiction on the down-low. Stories in *Triangulation, Clamour & Mischief, DreamForge,* and *Dark Cheer.*

Learn more here: https://linktr.ee/rjklee

20

MEMO FROM THE JOLLY OVERLORDS

BY R.J.K. LEE

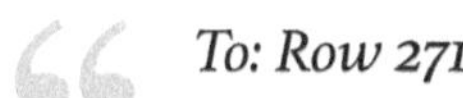

To: Row 271

Be advised: meet your daily quota. Miss it again and your row will be summoned for interrogation and review. Make the workshop proud this season.

~

Crumpling the memo into a ball, Stosh glared at the red overhead display: quota success pending.

As Worker A at the head of the conveyor belt, he took the initiative. "Worry not! An hour before we clock out. Twenty left on the table. Three minutes per toy. We can get it done together."

Ironic chuckles erupted from his pitiful fellows in their required bodysuits and hairnets. Stosh shrugged them off as inevitable. Everyone felt the despair. When he called his wife from his cubicle cot last night, she complained that their twins whimpered for more food.

They had to do better or their families suffered.

Stosh shaped plastic lumps into plump heads and bodies, then passed the dolls on to the next team members for limbs and accessories.

A messenger elf scurried from a hole behind Stosh. Loyal to the overlords, messengers were never gingersnap nice.

The muscled fellow in dirt-smeared green overalls squeezed Stosh's arm. "You losers are too bony for my taste."

He dropped another twenty plastic lumps onto the table then returned to the hollowed tunnels to the offices secreted within. The slapping and scratching sounds of climbers were a constant reminder of impatient activity.

With lumps in hand, Stosh addressed his team. "More from management. Twenty seconds per toy to meet quota."

They gaped, their bloodshot whites widened above dark, puffy circles, their ears drooping.

Stosh's neighboring teammate threw his toy limbs to the floor. "Impossible."

Rubbing his Adam's apple, Stosh knew his coworker was correct. With a spasm of fear, he stumbled from his seat. Gnarled roots framed the entrance to the tunnels. He pounded on the wood.

The loudspeaker crackled. "Return to your seat, Worker A. Quota demands attention."

His teammates stumbled from their seats in solidarity.

"Into the hole!"

The waifs of Row 271 puttered forward and climbed toward the offices, the overlords, and dreams of escape.

21

ABOUT "THE NEW MUTANTS"

First published: June 2020
Gotta Wear Eclipse Glasses by Third Flatiron Publishing

It's the End of the World and obviously time for an enormous rock concert. Lord of the Flies meets Station Eleven in this tale of masks and musical mayhem. This story won a Tangent Online Recommended Read in 2020.

22

THE NEW MUTANTS

BY ANGELIQUE FAWNS

Who knew when the world remade itself it would be one big Battle of the Bands? Before "the event," I avoided crowded concerts like the plague. But now crowds were at least one thing I didn't have to worry about anymore. In my previous life, I was a book-worm introvert. I avoided human interaction, and abhorred violence. To survive in our musical new world, I learned to make connections with others and embrace the bloodthirsty bit of lizard brain that lurked in my prefrontal cortex. Evolve (or perhaps de-evolve?) or die.

I was enjoying the cool night with my bestie Jay, rocking out to discordant music which matched the dismal landscape around us. Burned-out grass, a few trees in the throes of losing their last leaves, and a shanty town of plywood forts. A blanket with only a few holes provided a bit of warmth in the cool fall air. Our masks, which clearly labelled us as followers of The New Mutants, sat on the ground beside us. They were neon green plastic scrounged from one of the Dollar Stores still standing in the city. We added small goat horns with superglue, and the result was weird and intimidating. To think I used to find ripped jeans a bold fashion choice.

I cuddled into Jay, and let the throb of the punk rock song roll over me. The New Mutants were a six-member band, four guys and two gals, all heavily pierced with shredded leather outfits and copious metal jewellery.

"Hey lover boy," I murmured to the thin muscular guy beside me, putting my lips close to his ear to be heard above the screeching guitars, "do you think we will have an attack-free night, or am I going to have to try out my new cudgel?"

He pulled his battle-scarred body up and moved away from the forty or so New Mutant followers gathered on the grass. Shoving his dark hair out of the way, he cupped a hand over one ear and listened intently.

Walking back, he plopped down beside me, "Okay Aggie, I think I can hear some twang and harmonica from the east, The Cowboy Bangers might have a go at us tonight. God, I hate country music. Might be exciting to take a few of those boot-knockers down."

I didn't know Jay before. . . I could imagine him as a nerd, probably president of the chess club. He has a wonderfully strategic mind, but instead of moving pawns and queens, he spends his time figuring out how to keep us alive. We are both in our late teens, and should be worrying about what to wear to prom, not how to survive the night.

I picked up my brand-new weapon, a piece of stocky wood with long fence nails protruding from it. At our last battle with Slang Slinger, a Hip-Hop band with around fifty members who wore bandannas over their faces instead of actual masks, my baseball bat had broken when I hit a particularly large fellow. He'd been coming after me with a rifle. Ammunition was almost impossible to find, so he was using it as a club. It was part of the Slang Slinger image to use actual guns as weapons, even if they couldn't fire them.

When Jay saw I was weaponless, he grabbed me, and we ran before my enormous adversary could get back up. Dodging blows and weaving through other fights, we hid in the backseat of a burned-out Jeep on the edge of the battlefield. Listening to the cries and screams outside as Jay hunkered down on top of me, I closed my eyes and thought of my favorite memory, my last day before the world as we knew it ended.

It was the week before the Fowl Plague decimated the population. Frosh week at George Brown College in Toronto was full of parties, and I was so excited about my first year in Library Sciences. The famous Canadian band Blue Rodeo was performing at Sugar Beach.

Then my best, and only, friend Rebecca mentioned that a rare bird flu had killed a few people in Vancouver. We had no idea what was coming. They didn't shut down the airports in time. The virus killed within 24 hours. Within a week almost everyone I knew was dead, including all my family members.

It seemed only a few in their early 20's were immune. Rebecca and I were lucky to get out of the city before true madness hit. We took refuge in a cottage her parents owned on a lake a few hours north of the city. We managed by cutting firewood, hunting deer, and foraging for edible plants. But then one day—a few months later—Rebecca went out to gather fiddleheads and didn't return. I spent weeks scrounging the woods and looking for her body in the lake, but I couldn't find a single trace of her. I can't believe I used to read post-apocalyptic fiction for fun, living the reality was worse than any nightmare. Too devastated to stay in her cottage alone, I hit the road and walked south towards the city.

Two years later I was hiding in a useless vehicle (gas has run out long ago), a completely different person from that timid wallflower hoping to become a librarian. I never saw "feral fighter" in my tea leaves. After the fight died down and the last of the Slang Slinger members staggered back to their territory, we ventured out. Jay hunted around for materials to make me a new weapon, he had been an engineering intern at a Nuclear Power Plant, and along with having a strategic brain, he could design and create things. I helped bandage up the injured. In retrospect, I wish I had enrolled in nursing schooling. Not much need for organizing literature and procuring audiovisual inventory in my new life. However being able to mop up blood and stitch wounds was in high demand. Luckily no one had been killed in that skirmish, but there were lots of wounded.

Would we be as lucky tonight? I smiled as I heard my favorite song starting up, "Alien Rage." It was always the last song of The New Mutants set. Our entire group shuffled off the grass and went over to our campfire to share cans of soup and SPAM from our last looting venture. It took several days to complete an expedition down to Toronto for supplies. The food was probably why Slang Slinger attacked, it was getting harder and harder to find anything left in the grocery stores, and even residential homes. I used to have a soft body with a few rolls around my middle. Now I could count every rib with muscling lacing down my arms and legs.

Murder and mayhem ruled in the cities. Joining a band as a follower was the best way to survive. At least there was a code of behaviour and understanding between gangs. Skirmishes were supposed to be non-fatal, and more about territory, food, and status. If the Cowboy Bangers were coming after us tonight, it wasn't because they needed dinner. They had well-protected grain stores after being smart and raiding farm silos instead of relying on urban stores and homes. Their masks were the most terrifying of all. They used the skin off slaughtered pigs and strung coyote fangs around their cowboy hats. If that band showed up, it was just because they enjoyed a good fight.

"Jay, did you hear that?" I paused in my soup sipping.

I thought I could hear the faint notes of multiple strumming banjos. Most of our group was gathered around the band members, gushing about how amazing the music was that night. Jay and I sat on the periphery. I wasn't really a fan of punk rock music, but could pretend to enjoy anything to survive. Classical music used to be more my style.

Jay pushed his unruly black hair off his ears, "Yup. The Cowboy Bangers are looking to mix it up again tonight."

Originally, I had been a member of the Garden Gnomes, a folk music group who made their masks from flowers and tree sap. It was the first band gang who invited me in after I headed south from the cottage. That's where I met Jay. We immediately recognized the antisocial nerd tendencies in each other, and formed a bond. I loved the music and learned to love Jay, but we quickly realized the pot-smoking pacifists were poor fighters. After each skirmish, we had less food, and morale was dropping. When the New Mutants attacked us, we grabbed two masks off felled members and followed them back to their camp. Then we begged to join. I had learned to be persuasive and convinced the lead band members that our battle skills would offset any food we consumed. And by then the both of us had learned to fight. Jay and I shared dark stories about those whom we killed in the days before we found bands to join. A different kind of foreplay.

Over the crest of the hill, I could see the trademark cowboy hats and pitchforks heading towards us. The duelling banjo beat was getting closer. Our lookout high up in a tree noticed and banged a warning on the bass drum strung up in the branches. Our fellow New Mutants scrambled, shoving on masks and grabbing weapons. Jay poked me and pointed in the other direction. Rapping and bouncing to their own beat, Slang Slingers was also on the way. The other teenagers started to stir, picking up masks and weapons.

"This is going to get bloody," I gasped.

From the last remaining direction, I saw the worst gang of them all. The Neon Demons were a pure rock band and nasty fighters. They preferred knives and leering clown masks, and they had the highest injury ratio of them all. They actually took prisoners, even though that was supposed to be against the unspoken band war rules. Some members had guitars that they whacked and strummed as they marched.

"Remember, stay close to me, back-to-back, and let's stay near the edge so we can run if this gets too ugly," Jay screamed at me over the clashing sounds of the war marching music.

I took deep breaths and went into a zone of almost meditation-like stillness. Complete focus and awareness of my surrounding. Adrenaline enlivening my limbs and sharpening my senses.

In the next second it started. Screams and punches as the four gangs converged. I dodged blows and swung my cudgel, feeling blood spray across my mask, and I could hear Jay grunting behind me as he wielded his nunchucks. In the mayhem the only way to tell who belonged to what group were the hideous masks. If I saw plastic green, I held back my hits. Clowns, pigs, and bandannas I swung at aggressively.

The smell of sweat, coppery blood, and dirty body stung my nostrils. This was by far the worst brawl I had been in. I felt a pitchfork graze my thigh, and Jay shoved me aside and whacked at the Cowboy. Falling to the ground, I could see sneakers with holes, scuffed cowboy boots, and skinny scabbed legs. I could hear grunts and profanity as I waited for a gun, pitchfork or knife to land.

A large boom shattered the air, and a huge white flash lit up the battleground. Everyone froze as the ground shook beneath us. Masks fell as we all turned and watched the sky lighting up to the west.

I heard someone beside me ask, "did a bomb hit?"

Someone else, "that looks like a mushroom cloud. How close are we to the Nuclear Power Plant?"

The voice was familiar. I turned and saw blonde hair and button nose. A clown mask dangled from one hand.

"Rebecca! Is that you?"

Disbelief, joy, and shock. Three emotions I hadn't felt for a while, much less simultaneously.

"Aggie! I never thought I would see you again," she wiped some blood off her face and engulfed me in a big hug. "I was kidnapped and taken by the Neon Demons. I'm so sorry I couldn't get back to you!"

I sobbed into her hair, "I'm so thankful you are alive."

Around me, other gang members were also discovering lost friends as the glow from the explosion illuminated our unmasked faces. We only ever mingled with other bands with our masks on. There was no social interaction off the battle field.

Between hugs and hand shaking, I could hear everyone wondering if it was the nuclear power plant and what that meant for us. Pretty unlikely it was a bomber. No planes had flown for years. Were our days numbered? Was radiation going to kill the rest of us?

"How long do you think we have if that was the nuclear plant?" I asked Jay, who had joined in the big embrace with Rebecca. He had heard many of my stories about Rebecca in the long hours we spent together and wiped tears away more than a few times.

"Our Candu reactors are far too stable. This explosion looks to me like a warship or a cargo ship carrying something flammable just went up on Lake Ontario."

Jay's days as an intern at the power plant made him the only one who might have a useful opinion. He used to brag that Canada was years ahead with their clean energy plan and nuclear safety standards.

"I sure don't want to spend my last days fighting," I could hear a Cowboy Banger saying to a Slang Slinger next to us.

I whispered to Jay and Rebecca, "let them think it's the nuclear reactor and these are our last days. It might mean peace between the bands!"

We turned and watched people dropping their masks in the dirt. Cowboy Bangers hugged Neon Demons, and Slang Slingers shook hands with New Mutants.

Our lead singer hopped up on our makeshift stage and hollered out over the crowd, "If this is truly the end, let's go out with the biggest concert of all times!"

The crowd of bloodied teenagers started a slow clap. This was something I never thought I'd see outside of a movie. A Cowboy Banger jumped up on the stage with her and started a cool riff with his banjo. Then a Neon Demon picked up a bass guitar, and a throbbing harmony rang out over the grass.

The lead singer of the Slang Slingers hopped up, chanting, "It's the end of the world as we know it. The Nuclear Plant just got lit. Let's throw down our weapons for peace, and show Woodstock how we do it in the east."

Hugging Rebecca and Jay, I swayed back and forth to the music. More people were jumping up on stage, or just picking up an instrument and joining in where they stood. This was the best music I had heard in years, and Jay grinned from ear-to-ear and knocked his nunchucks together to the beat.

By our New Mutant campfire pit, I could see a huge flame roaring. Gang members danced over and threw their masks in the fire. I picked up our two green masks and Rebecca's clown face, walked over to the fire, and tossed them in. Then I went back and sat down with my friends in the grass to enjoy the music.

23

ABOUT "REMEMBER THE GALLSCREAM"

n Original Story for Cursed & Creepy

CHRISTOPHER HENCKEL IS a guest author in this collection, and the bizarre characters at this spooky carnival will stretch even the most pliable of imaginations.

BORN in the backwoods of West Virginia, Christopher Henckel is a country boy down to his molecular structure. He now lives in New Zealand with his lovely partner, Annaliese, and two equally lovely daughters, Avery and Coco. His stories can be found in Galaxy's Edge magazines and various anthologies. When he's not writing, Henckel works as a Senior Procurement Specialist for the NZ Government.

24

REMEMBER THE GALLSCREAM

BY CHRISTOPHER HENCKEL

*B*y the time Scarecrow saw the neon sign flickering above the carnival's gates, it was too late. Dark creatures crowded him armed with sparklers, balloons, and glow-in-the-dark necklaces. But it wasn't their high-pitched giggles or careless use of firecrackers that worried him. It was the sign, which read: *Remember the Gallscream.*

Scarecrow rubbed the straw bristling at the back of his neck. "Maybe we should go somewhere else."

His teenage daughter, Darkling, rolled her painted eyes and yanked him forward in the queue. "Don't wimp out on me. You promised."

"What, me? I'm not wimping out. I'm just thinking, we should do something else."

Something that doesn't involve this carnival. Anything, actually.

Darkling looked like her mother. Her face was pale canvas with dark hollowed eyes and a lovely gash of crimson for a mouth. Her lanky straw legs she'd gotten from Scarecrow, but the studded dog collar necklace and slouch beany pulled cocked over one eye was her own.

She crossed her arms and huffed. Scarecrow felt the distance between them grow. It was heartbreaking.

The crowd pushed forward, moving Scarecrow and Darkling closer to the front of the queue.

"How about we go buy that hatchet you've been wanting?" Scarecrow asked, more desperate than ever. "Sharp enough to sever an arm and still keep an edge."

"Right now?" Darkling asked.

"Sure. My treat. Come on."

Scarecrow stepped from the queue, relief already flooding through him. But Darkling didn't follow him.

"You don't want to go to the carnival with me," she said, dropping her gaze to trawl through the weeds between her feet.

Scarecrow knew he'd screwed up. The distance between him and Darkling had always existed, but the last few months had been the worst. It seemed the harder he tried to mend the gap, the more Darkling pushed him away. That's why he proposed they go to the carnival tonight: one last-ditch effort to salvage their relationship.

Of course, that was before he noticed the sign.

For most creatures, *Gallscream* was a supernatural being that appeared ten years ago. But for Scarecrow, the reference was dangerous. There was more to the night of the Gallscream than Darkling knew, and those details would be hidden in every corner of this silly carnival. Details Scarecrow would stop at nothing to hide from Darkling.

Preferably in a way that didn't widen the gap between them.

"Nonsense," Scarecrow said.

"Then why are you so determined to leave?"

"Mildew infection," he said, clamping his knees together. "It itches bad."

"Gross," Darkling said.

Inside the ticket booth an enormous toad perched precariously on a narrow stool. He drew from a sausage-sized cigar and then blew smoke from the corner of his mouth. "Two adults? That'll be twenty bucks," he said.

Scarecrow froze, like a deer in headlights. If Scarecrow left now, his and Darkling's fractured relationship would erode beyond repair. But if they went inside, and Darkling discovered the truth, then what remained of their fragile relationship would shatter like glass.

Unless, Scarecrow rationalized with a flurry of excitement, *I can bring her inside the carnival but steer her away from certain details.*

"What's it gonna be, Pal?" The toad croaked and drew again from his stubby cigar. "You coming or not?"

Scarecrow handed the toad twenty dollars with shaking hands. Then, with more confidence than he felt, he said to Darkling, "Come on. You and me kid-o. Let's have fun."

THE CARNIVAL WAS a calamity of corrugated iron and rickety ruins. Flakes of rust fluttered from the Ferris wheel, flickering like gold dust as they fell. The air smelled like hot funnel cakes and sickly-sweet cotton candy. Children threw daggers at a scampering clown, and vendors sold tinctured punch and fermented ice cream.

"Long live the Gallscream," a vendor volleyed for Scarecrow's attention.

Scarecrow nodded politely, intending to move along, but Darkling stopped, echoing the vendor's sentiment. "Long live the Gallscream."

The vendor was a mongoose with a mohawk and tartan kilt. His mohawk was blood-red at its base and worked its way up through the colors of the rainbow, ending in aquamarine. Before him, a trestle table lay bare except for three identical plastic cups. These he lifted, revealing a single piece of gray shale, which he flicked between the cups.

"The Gallscream be a particular hero of mine. Clever he was." The mongoose released the cups and spread his stubby arms. "Choose."

Darkling pointed to the cup in the middle. The mongoose lifted it, but the gray shale had vanished.

"Keep your eye on the stone, young miss," the mongoose said, and they played again.

Scarecrow turned his attention toward the ice cream stand in the next stall and the twin tiger cubs tugging urgently on their mother's apron.

"Please, Mom," the cubs said. "Just one ice cream. We can share it."

Their mother, a frail-looking tigress in a rag tunic, clawed open her purse and then shook her head. Her cubs, apparently well-tutored in disappointment, nuzzled her without further plea or protest.

"That's okay," they said.

Scarecrow glanced around to see if anyone was watching. Seeing no one, he drew upon on his shallow supply of magic, suggesting to the tub of ice cream that it would rest more comfortably if it were in the paws of the tiger cubs.

Scarecrow's magic was a secret, and many years had passed since he'd used it. Deeply in concentration, he watched the tub of ice cream rise from the parlor. It wobbled in mid-air, then it fell with a thud back into its former position.

Scarecrow cursed. At the height of his powers, he could control twenty objects at once. It saddened him to know how the years had eroded his powers away. Of course, he could have all his powers back; but like all things in life, there was a cost.

Scarecrow fetched two coins from his pocket and flicked them to the cubs. He mouthed the words *ice cream* to them and watched them dance exuberantly.

Behind Scarecrow, the mongoose said, "Don't be discouraged, lass. Because everyone be winners tonight. For I know everything about the Gallscream and the night he slew the humans. 'Tis me passion, you see. Now, go on, ask me anything."

Darkling sucked her cheek. "Do you know the name Abigail S. Crow?" she said.

The Mongoose scratched at his mohawk, and then he laughed. "Ah yes. She be scarecrow lady who be killed by the humans that night. And if I be judging rightly, you be the wee Darkling found buried beneath her in the cornfield."

This vignette t-boned Scarecrow's senses with the force of a train. He flinched into the table, toppling it. Passersby turned to stare. Scarecrow caught Darkling by the arm and fled.

"Come on," he said. "I smell funnel cakes."

They weaved through the crowd, past a pig in short pants dancing and playing his pipes, and beyond him was a badger in a bikini bobbing for apples in a wooden barrel.

They stopped outside a candle maker's tent when Darkling yanked her arm free and cocked her hip to one side.

"What was that all about?" she said.

"What do you mean?" Scarecrow said.

"I mean, the mongoose. That was so rude of you."

"Was it?"

"Yes!"

"I'm sorry. I just got worked up, listening to him bleat about stuff he doesn't know anything about. He talked about you and your mom as if he was some authority, but his facts were all wrong."

Darkling's glare melted. "I wondered about that," she said.

"Well, wonder no longer," Scarecrow said. "Because I was there that night with you and your mom. And we weren't anywhere near some silly cornfield."

"I guess so."

"I know so. And that mongoose back there doesn't have a clue."

Darkling accepted the lie without further protest, and Scarecrow felt equal parts shame and relief.

THEY WALKED until they came to a squirrel with a tie-dyed tail and dreadlocked fur. The squirrel swallowed fire and burped a blaze. The fur around his tiny mouth was singed from the flames and his two front teeth were black as soot.

When the performance ended, Darkling clapped and cheered.

The squirrel wiped his mouth on his furry forearm then gave Darkling and Scarecrow each a high-five.

"Long live the Gallscream, dudes," the squirrel said. "You liked the show?"

Darkling rose on her toes and tapped her fingers together in a miniature applause. "That was amazing. But doesn't it hurt?"

"Nothing a little lip balm and some antiseptic can't fix." The squirrel patted his hemp satchel, which he wore across his body. "Anyway, my name is Blaze, and fire is my forte. Tonight, I pay homage to the twenty-seven creatures whose homes were burnt by the humans, the night the Gallscream came."

"Twenty-seven?" Darkling said, eyes widening.

Scarecrow nodded absently, but his attention shifted to a tiny tamarin monkey swinging along the fringes of a nearby tent. The tamarin clutched a red balloon in its teeth, and it moved with the skill of an acrobat. When the tamarin saw Scarecrow, it smiled. The balloon's string pulled from between the gap in the creature's teeth like dental floss and floated far from the tamarin's reach.

Again, Scarecrow glanced around to see if anyone was watching him. Confident the coast was clear, he broadcasted a cognitive message to the balloon, suggesting that its ascension was irrational given its tremendous weight.

The red balloon ceased to rise. It shuddered at this alien force, popped, and fell limply amongst popcorn and paper cups scattered across the ground.

The tiny tamarin sagged at the sight of its sorry balloon, turned tail, and ran away weeping.

Scarecrow closed his eyes and shook his head. Such magic was once child's play for him. Technically, it could be again, but he'd sworn to never draw from the pool again.

He turned his attention back toward Darkling and the squirrel and found them deep in conversation.

"Seriously, I'm one hundred percent sure of that." Blaze retrieved his flask of kerosene from his satchel and swirled it like a martini.

"The humans never made it north of the river. That's why only the houses in the south were burnt."

Scarecrow felt his panic rise.

"Nonsense, the humans were all over the place that night." Scarecrow nudged Darkling to keep moving. "Come on. I'm parched. Let's grab a soda."

The squirrel folded his furry arms like tiny twigs twisting together. "I know my history, dude."

"Your history is as patchy as your fur, pyro-rat."

Scarecrow would have said more, but Darkling disappeared into the crowd, and he was forced to jog to catch up.

"Hey, wait up," he said. "Let's grab those sodas now, or maybe some funnel cakes."

Darkling whirled on Scarecrow. "Why have you been lying to me?"

"What do you mean?"

"Don't play dumb."

"What, you mean those idiots?" Scarecrow jerked his head back in the direction of the mongoose and squirrel then forced a laugh. "They're probably reading from the same hatchet-job history book. I swear the education system nowadays is appalling."

Darkling frowned at him. "You're hiding something," she said.

"No, I'm not."

"Then why doesn't anything make sense?"

"Darkling, what could I possibly have to hide?"

She shot him a mistrusting glare. "Then swear it," she said. "Swear it on Mom's grave, that you're telling me the truth."

A rogue breeze blew past, carrying the sickly-sweet scent of cotton candy and buttery popcorn. Scarecrow's mouth felt very dry.

"Of course," he lied. "I swear it."

The downward slope of Darkling's shoulders and her heavy-lidded, painted eyes made her look tired.

"Fine," she said, and the matter was put to rest.

Yet, deep inside Scarecrow, he knew good fathers didn't lie to their daughters. Even if it was for their own good.

SCARECROW BOUGHT funnel cakes and sodas for himself and Darkling. They ate in an amphitheater while watching a reenactment of the night the Gallscream came, played by five monkeys in matted motley.

The monkey playing the part of the Gallscream stood at one end of the stage shrouded in shadows. Two more assumed the roles of the dark creatures. The last two played the part of the humans. On a high level, the reenactment was true enough. The humans came and burned the dark creatures' homes. Those creatures who resisted were slaughtered.

Scarecrow didn't need a reenactment to remind him of that night. He'd been there and relived the events in his nightmares hundreds of times over. He remembered the flames flickering in the darkness and the scent of smoke smoldering from thatch roofs. He remembered feeling hopeless and helpless and angry.

That's when the Gallscream appeared: the supernatural savior that no one knew or had heard of until that night. Shrouded in mist and shadows, the Gallscream was terrible to behold. A monolithical beast, rising from the shadows, with a piercing scream that sent humans and creatures to tremble. The humans covered their ears and ran away screaming. But none escaped. The Gallscream chased them down. Using his never-before-seen supernatural powers, he animated twenty daggers, which he slung and whipped from human to human until all were dead.

Then the Gallscream disappeared, never to be seen or heard of again.

For many creatures, this was the beginning and end of the story. But for Scarecrow, there was more.

All I ever wanted was to be a good dad. But now he wondered if his lie was to protect Darkling or himself? If the latter, then all his lies were selfish. *What kind of father does that?*

The reenactment ended and the crowd applauded the actors. Scarecrow folded his funnel cake into its paper plate, untouched, then clapped too.

He and Darkling meandered behind the crowd in a state of automation, his gaze downcast.

"Can we talk?" he said.

They sat together beneath the rusty Ferris wheel on a bench where the green paint peeled around a festering patch of rot. Scarecrow picked at the peeling paint as he spoke.

"I've not been honest with you," he said. "But you deserve the truth."

"What is it?"

"It's about your mom."

Darkling leaned forward on the bench, resting her elbows on her knees. "I'm listening," she said.

Scarecrow drew a deep, brave breath and told his secret. "You, your mother, and I weren't at home that night. We were in the cornfield. That's when we saw the humans. They were senselessly killing defenseless creatures. Your mother demanded that we run away together. But I said that running was too dangerous. I said we needed to stay put, hide in the corn, then maybe they wouldn't see us. Cradling you in her arms, your mother did as I asked. The humans moved toward us, but they didn't see us. I began to think we were safe. After a while, I told your mom the coast was clear, and it was safe to go home. But I was wrong."

He paused to take several deep breaths.

"When they caught Abigail, she covered you with her own body, so they wouldn't see you. She saved your life. Not me."

The carnival's music changed, and in the space between the old and the new was an electric void that thrummed hollowly in the atmosphere.

Darkling drew in a deep breath and then released it with quavering exhalation. "You abandoned us?" she said.

"Yes."

"Mom's dead because of you."

"Yes, but there's more. Please listen."

"I've heard enough."

"No, you need to hear the next part."

"I don't need the next anything." Darkling rose and batted the remains of her father's funnel cake and soda from his hands. The soda splashed his pants, and she screamed. "You're such a liar! I hate you!"

She fled deeper into the carnival, shouldering creatures from her path. Scarecrow called to her, but she didn't turn back. He couldn't blame her. He was, beyond any shadow of a doubt, the worst father that ever lived.

A SCREECH of metal-on-metal cut through the festivities, and then two ice creams splattered at Scarecrow's feet. Somebody screamed and everyone looked up at the seat hanging precariously from the top of the Ferris wheel. Its weight, now uneven, caused the wheel to lean to the point of toppling. The creatures in the lower seats jumped free, thumping onto the ground. But there were still two creatures clinging to the top.

The twin cubs wailed and scrambled onto the crossbeams. Their seat fell, slamming against the Ferris wheel, causing it to lean further.

"Climb down, mates," a kangaroo said, but the cubs didn't come.

"Someone's got to save them," a snake hissed.

"Can't. Any more weight and them youngins gonna fall," a coon dog said.

The mother tigress burst from the crowd, her eyes focused with predatorial, maternal instinct. She braced her shoulder against the wheel and strained. Her veins rose like taut ropes as she fought to right the leaning Ferris wheel, and she was joined by a migration of supporters who also put their shoulders to the wheel.

"Hold on," the tigress called. "Hold on. You'll be okay."

But in Scarecrow's mind, these were not the words of the tigress. These were the words of his wife, as she hunched over in the cornfield, protecting her newborn Darkling as the humans burnt her alive.

Hold on. You'll be okay.

But she'd been wrong. Help had come too late.

It had been seeing Abigale burned alive that changed Scarecrow into the Gallscream. But it was too little, too late. The Gallscream may have saved dozens of dark creatures that night, but he'd failed to protect his own family. That was Scarecrow's shame. And that is why he swore to never become the Gallscream again.

Until now.

Forgive me, Abigail.

For the first time in more than a decade, Scarecrow transformed. The darkness lingering beneath the benches and tucked tightly in the folds of flapping canvas crept free. It swam like eels a foot above the ground. It passed the creatures, vendors, and vans. It circled the seats in front of the stage, and it gathered like a whirlpool at Scarecrow's feet.

Inside that swirling mist, Scarecrow ceased to be. In his place, rising like an ancient monolithic shrine was the Gallscream.

The Ferris wheel was far too massive for the Gallscream to hold with his mind. So, he focused on small things—the plastic cups from the mongoose's table, the flask and lip balm from the squirrel's hemp satchel, the tiny tamarin's tangerine balloon, and the tubs of fermented ice cream inside the dented white van. He focused on these plus a thousand more items just like them. He pushed his mind to the limits, then he re-doubled his efforts, arranging the items into a rickety staircase that rose to the top of the Ferris wheel.

This strain felt like a jagged rasp shaving layers off his mind, each mental stroke forcing a few more pieces to fall from the stairs.

"Get them," the Gallscream said. "I can't hold ... much longer ..."

The figure that took up the call was small—no larger than a teenager. She wore a black tee-shirt, a studded dog collar necklace, and a slouch beanie that covered one eye.

Darkling darted up the stairs as the pieces fell away. At the top, she gathered the cubs in her arms and then raced back down. But by then, the Gallscream's mind collapsed under the strain.

The final images burned in his mind were of the debris falling from under Darkling's feet, of her leaping, two steps at a time, with the tiny cubs cradled under each arm, and of her falling from very high up.

~

THE GALLSCREAM FADED, and Scarecrow reappeared. His awareness opened to the pain of a broken heart and an aching head. Dark creatures surrounded him, whispering reverently. They did not touch him.

Yards away, the tigress in the rag tunic clutched her cubs and wept into their scruffy fur. The cubs squalled and retaliated against her embrace and were unharmed.

Beyond them, Darkling lay on the ground, curled into a ball and trembling amidst a scattering of trampled popcorn and disposable paper cups. She cradled one arm, and her right leg was bent in the wrong direction. She cried silently into the debris.

Scarecrow gathered her in his arms, and he carried her back toward the gates. The closeness of their bodies diminished, if only briefly, the vast space between them.

The veil of night faded, and soon the sky was a glassy sheen of marbled navy and tangerine. The carnival's neon lights ceased to flicker, and the rapid-fire music gave way to starlings perched on the carnival's gates.

Scarecrow and Darkling left the carnival, their shadows stretching before them.

Whatever came next, forgiveness or otherwise, was in Darkling's hands. If she forgave Scarecrow, it would be in her own time and on her own terms. Scarecrow resolved to wait. He would love her regardless and be completely honest with her—because that's what a good dad does.

25

ABOUT "MINNY AND THE MUTANT TOMATO"

*a*n Original Story for Cursed & Creepy

I ATTENDED *my first writing retreat on Pelee Island. The rich soil, the remote location, the intense farming operations... A perfect setting for some strangeness.*

26

MINNY & THE MUTANT TOMATO

BY ANGELIQUE FAWNS

Minny Brown skipped through her father's tomato field on Pelee Island, her face warm from the June sun. She clenched the shovel in her hands, palms sweaty with purpose. She loved the tangy smell of the green shoots in the rich, fertilized field. Even the pungent manure smelled like freedom from the drudgery of school.

Her pocket bulged from a little bottle labelled "growth formula" she'd stolen from her father's farm office. Her cheeks were flushed from the thrill of the heist, and she felt a little sick to her stomach. Like last year when she ate too much cotton candy at the Leamington Fair. Minny didn't like to cheat or misbehave, but she hated not winning.

She wrinkled her nose with the memory of last year's horrible fair. Not only had she puked behind the Ferris wheel from the cotton candy, but she'd lost the youth "Biggest Tomato" competition to Farley from the next farm over. Purple rage made her shiver. The stocky boy liked to catch her behind the school and pull on her dark curls.

The bottle dug into her hip, causing intermittent flashes of discomfort. She was wearing her favorite overalls for bravery, even though they were getting tight in the butt and chest. She adjusted the stolen vial and grimaced. Dad said she was "becoming a woman." Gag.

Minny suspected this was why Farley had stopped torturing toads and focused on her now. It also meant this was her last year to win. Once you turned thirteen, you had to compete in the teen division.

Minny dropped the shovel and fell to her knees where the vines twisted highest towards the sky. With trembling fingers, she pulled out the iridescent powder. Was it her imagination, or were the contents moving? Blurring and wiggling like her vision on the Tilt-A-Whirl? She hesitated--

But then she pictured Farley's sneering face as he waved his blue ribbon last year. (He won with an enormous yellow Heirloom tomato.) With a quick twist of her wrist, she dumped half the granules on the roots of the biggest plant and screwed the lid back on.

She waited.

Nothing.

A drop of sweat dribbled down her nose, and she noticed a soupy smell coming from her T-shirt. Her mom was right. She had to try deodorant. This growing older was annoying. So was watching this dang tomato plant. Nothing was happening. Her stomach sank like a roller coaster and she picked up her shovel to head for a shower.

She heard a gurgle, sort of like the Christmas turkey at feeding time. She turned and her jaw dropped.

The thick dark soil bubbled like the leftover turkey soup as the plant vibrated and shot up a foot. The green leaves unfurled and reached for the sky. Minny gasped. Forget Jack's magic beans, this plant was GROWING.

A ginormous tomato blew up like a balloon and dropped to the ground. It was bigger than the stuffed toy she won at Whack-A-Mole! She wrinkled her nose when she picked it up. It was slimy and warm.

"Hey easy there, kid, you're going to bruise me," the tomato said in a voice full of gravel.

Minny shrieked and dropped the fruit. She backed up a few steps. What was in that powder?

The tomato quivered and dark pupil-less eyes blinked. "Bull patties, that will leave a mark."

It scowled at her with a mouth that took up fully half of his face. Little fangs shone in the early afternoon sun.

"You talk?" Minny squeaked, crouching to get a better look. She was very careful not to touch him. "What's your name?"

He rolled and his orange skin caught the sun. "I'm Tom. Tom the tomato. What else would I be called?" He glistened with a visceral goo.

"Did I hurt you?" Minny reached to touch the tomato man. "I don't see any bruises, except those two bumps."

The tomato rolled back a foot. "Those are my ears, don't be poking them."

"Sorry!" She held her hands up. "I'm Minny. I was hoping to enter you in the fall fair. Not sure what division you belong in, now."

"I got stuff to do." Tom spit with mirth, a gooey orange blob. "No time for fairs for this fruit."

She tilted her head. "So, what am I supposed to do with you?"

Tom gnashed his sharp, pointed teeth. "It's about what you can do for me."

Minny felt a churning in her belly. Like the last few sticky bites of cotton candy were stuck to the roof of her mouth.

Tom's eyes gleamed. "You've got arms, Minny. I don't."

Minny gulped. The tomato had grown more since he dropped off the vine. Tom was currently the size of a truck tire.

He rolled around her, getting slightly larger with every rotation. "I'd like to make myself a sweet companion. A real cute tomato if you will."

Minny felt a bolt of fear flash up her spine. "What?"

Tom butted her thigh where the bottle sat in her pocket. "You put something on my roots, didn't you?"

The warm squishy feel of his flesh on her leg made her skin crawl. She nodded, her brain racing.

"Take your powder." He nodded to a plant with a tiny green tomato hanging off the vine. "And make me a friend."

Minny lost herself in those dark eyes. Almost not of her own volition, she pulled out her bottle--

"Go on!" Tom spat.

With a trembling hand, she dumped the powder on the roots of the plant. It grew like the last one and the little fruit swelled and dropped off the vine.

Minny's head ached as she watched thick red lips form on the plump surface. Long lashes framed intelligent blinking blue eyes. The tomato hissed and long fangs sprouted vampirically from her rosebud mouth.

Tom hooted. "That's what I'm talking about. A real cutie-patootie!"

"The name is Thomasina. Not cutie-patootie." The new tomato scowled. "You overripe idiot."

Minny crawled backwards until her hand landed on her shovel.

Tom blinked. "Sorry honey. Ummm--"

Minny fought acid rushing up her throat as the female tomato bristled, sprouting green leaves from her head. She grew even faster than Tom. Both were the size of tractor tires now.

Minny inched the shovel closer to her side and pulled herself up on her knees.

The tomatoes were too busy arguing to pay attention to her.

Thomasina battered Tom with her leaves. "We need to make more of us. This could be our rich and tasty new world."

Minny thought she had felt terror in the fair Haunted House, but that was nothing compared to the fear freezing her veins now. Had she unleashed the sequel to the "Attack of the Killer Tomatoes" on Pelee Island?

Her hand, twice as sweaty as it was an hour ago, swung her shovel.

She squashed Thomasina, her seeds and liquid splattering on Tom's face. Minny's overalls became soaked in viscous goo.

Tom screamed as Minny raised the shovel again. His deep eyes met hers, but she knew she had to be cold and resolute. Like her mom with the holiday turkey. With a solid swing, she brought her shovel down on Tom's head.

He exploded in a rush of saucy red brine.

Minny gasped, her chest heaving. She stood in a puddle of red fluid, bits of tomato flesh spattered around her. Her nostrils flared as the acidic smell of mushed tomato mixed with body odor. Kind of like all-you-can-eat spaghetti night at the legion.

With a shudder, she dropped the shovel. So much for winning the largest tomato competition. Tears filled her eyes as she thought of Farley. He would win again.

A bit of tomato flesh stuck to her lip. She licked it off and a rush of delicious sweetness filled her mouth. Better than anything she'd ever eaten before.

"Yum." Her tongue flicked out to lick the last of it.

A smile lit up her flushed face. She might not win the biggest fruit this year, but these magic squashed tomatoes were tasty. She might have the tomato sauce competition on lock. Her new recipe would be a sure winner.

She took Dad's growth formula and tossed the empty bottle into the burn bin. She'd learned a lesson today. The only powder she'd be adding was garlic and salt.

ABOUT THE AUTHOR

Angelique Fawns loves to spin dark tales and is incredibly nosy. She takes her natural inclination to ask far too many questions and interviews publishers, editors, and authors for horrortree.com and her own blog at www.fawns.ca/blog.

She has a day job as a television producer and lives on a farm north of Toronto with her husband, daughter, horses, cats, and a rescued Potcake dog.

When she can find the time, she sneaks away to her Golden Falcon trailer by the river to do some writing. You can find her work in *Ellery Queen Mystery Magazine*, *DreamForge Anvil*, and on her podcast *Read Me A Nightmare*.

 facebook.com/amfawns
x.com/angeliquefawns
 instagram.com/angeliqueiswriting

BUT WAIT! THERE'S MORE...

**Enjoyed this book? Check out the others in the Horror Lite
Series!**

Peculiar Pets

Mythical Monsters

Like to Listen?

Read Me A Nightmare Podcast

Did you enjoy reading these dark quirky tales? Would you like to hear them
performed on a podcast? Look for *Read Me A Nightmare* wherever you get
your podcasts.

A writer yourself?

The Guide of All Guides

To learn more about selling your short stories and making money, I've created a guide to the best no-fee, paying markets.

The Guide of All Guides is a comprehensive list of publishers and podcasters buying speculative fiction, complete with secrets and insights.

****Sign Up for my newsletter at www.fawns.ca*

If you enjoyed the foreword of this book, I highly recommend you check out Mark Leslie's collection **Nocturnal Screams.**

https://books2read.com/b/mle5rv

THE MOST TERRIFYING THINGS HAPPEN IN THE DARK

Screams echo through the thick darkness of night in this collection of three short horror tales from the dark mind of Mark Leslie.